About the Author

Anna Lopes lives in Recife, Pernambuco, Brazil. She graduated with a major in Psychology and a minor in Creative Writing from Belhaven University in Mississippi, U.S. Anna has worked in a psychiatric hospital called Laurel Ridge Treatment Center in Texas, U.S., where her love for helping people only grew. She also likes cats, crime dramas, and mystery novels.

Comatose

Anna Lopes

Comatose

Olympia Publishers
London

www.olympiapublishers.com
OLYMPIA PAPERBACK EDITION

A CIP catalogue record for this title is available from the British Library.

ISBN: 978-1-80074-669-5

This is a work of fiction.
Names, characters, places and incidents originate from the writer's imagination. Any resemblance to actual persons, living or dead, is purely coincidental.

First Published in 2023

Olympia Publishers
Tallis House
2 Tallis Street
London
EC4Y 0AB

Printed in Great Britain

Dedication

To Shannon.

Acknowledgments

I owe great thanks to my creative writing teachers, Randy Smith and Howard Bahr, for teaching me how to excel in my writing. I would like to thank my parents for supporting me in writing this book and in everything else I do. I would also like to thank my two brothers (Sam and David), Paul Lang, Shannon Parker, Kristin Boes, Natalia Ferreira and Tatiana Menezes for reading my book and giving me insight on what was good and what needed editing. And I would also like to thank you, dear reader, for giving my story a voice.

Solstice

The silence in the carcass of these buildings urges me to get some sleep, but I'm stuck in this fire-bathed wasteland.

I've been here before. I can feel it in the dust, in the chaos of brick, cement, glass. Then the feeling dissipates.

That wasn't me. That was someone else. That was a luckier man, one who was allowed to love without boundaries, cling to life without regret.

The air is heavy, laced with a poison concocted for me, and I gasp it in and wait for daybreak.

Chapter 1

Alexandra did what she regularly did once a month: look for indie games at the thrift store. She flipped through the used, case-less videogame discs. She hummed variations of the Tetris theme song and rocked on her heels. The time was bordering 11.30 a.m., and the only others present were the pimply store worker and a big man making shuffling and grunting noises by the ceramics and pottery.

She ignored the generic game titles like *NFL Madden* and *Mario Kart*, and made note of ones like *Kinesis*, *Prosp and the End of Tomorrow*, *Comatose*, and *True Beef*. Her brother Ben was going to get at her for adding one more item to her collection of obscure videogames, but that made the endeavor even more worthwhile. *If an action has no external impact, it is not worth doing* was one of Alexandra's mantras. If the action affected her twin, it was better. He needed some affecting right now.

She was wearing a black, pleated skirt with dark red streaks and a frilly, red blouse. Her dark hair was done up in a messy bun. When she had left the apartment quickly and quietly to avoid waking her visiting brother, she had picked the first shoes she could find – neon-green sneakers. She sensed the teenage worker looking in her direction every other second. They locked gazes, and she gave him a death glare with her amber eyes. His face grew a shade redder than his pimples, and he lowered his head. She resumed her videogame browsing, satisfied.

Alexandra picked up two of them, smiled to herself, and took decisive strides toward the unsuspecting ceramics grunter. "May I trouble you for a while?" she asked him.

The man looked up from a tall-necked vase and gave her a blank stare. He wore glasses and a mullet. His face was mostly nose.

"I am indecisive," she said, lifting the games to his glasses, "between *Prosp and the End of Tomorrow* – which, from the disc cover, seems quite hearty – and *Comatose*, which has no image but the title itself. Which sparks your attention?"

The man sniffed through his big nose, pointed to the brisk lettering of *Comatose*, and resumed his vase examination. Alexandra smiled her thanks, went back to the used games, put *Prosp* back, and skipped to the front desk. The pimply young man backed away when she came close. From such close quarters, she noticed his nose-ring and Winnie-the-Pooh T-shirt: the yellow bear was munching on some strips of bacon. She grinned, carefully placed the game on the counter, and pointed to it.

"I will buy this today," she said.

The young man mumbled the price and put *Comatose* in a brown plastic bag.

It was noon when Alexandra parked her dark trail bike outside the apartment building.

She slipped her neon sneakers off. Held them in one hand. She had the plastic bag with the game bunched up in the other. Her breath held in anticipation, she walked up the old stairs to her flat. The eighth step was unforgivably squeaky. She kept to the corners as best she could. Alexandra placed her sneakers down with caution on the top landing.

The doorknob would not turn. Had she locked the door on her way out? She took her keys from one of the hidden pockets of her skirt and cradled them in one hand to keep them from jingling against each other, picked the right key, and turned it in the lock. The door snapped open. She silently cursed the noise. Alexandra tiptoed into the hallway, still holding the keys and plastic bag. Ben was asleep on the living room's wine-colored couch.

It amazed her how deathly still he looked when asleep. The window curtains were open, and light filtered through to his serene face, white pillow under his head. He slept with his hands behind his head, arms tight against his ears to shield them from any noise. Even so, he was a light sleeper. He faced the TV mounted on the opposite wall, his knees bent, curly dark hair partially covering his eyelids. He had not changed out of the blue jeans and grey shirt from the day before.

For the time he was spending with her between graduation and a job, he used her living room as his own space, and he monopolized the couch backed against the wall. He had some books lined up beside it, and Alexandra's life-size statue of a Roman soldier served as a bookend. He lived out of a large suitcase and a backpack, her Rembrandt above it. In front of the couch was her rickety table, and on top of it were his essentials; smartphone, wallet, car key on keychain, toothbrush, and an intricate tower of Sweet Tarts.

From where she stood at the end of the hallway, she saw her goal: the bedroom door. The space between table and TV wall was narrow, but it was the safest path to take: the floor was quieter there. Her wooden floorboards, though aesthetically pleasing, were no help when it came to sneaking. Her cotton socks countered that. She placed a confident foot forward and began her careful journey. Her gaze focused on Ben.

That morning, her lithe body had betrayed her as she stumbled over his dark shoes. He had stirred and almost woke. This time she was ready. She approached the table, stepped around the discarded shoes, tiptoed around the table, past the TV. She saw her copy of Van Gogh's self-portrait in her peripherals. She was almost to safety and the feeling of success was palpable.

She tripped on something soft and reached for the wall beside her to keep balance. Her keys fell to the ground and her fingers brushed Van Gogh. The portrait fell to her feet with a clatter. She picked up the stuffed rhinoceros – the cause of her failure – and looked at it, trying to hide her feelings of defeat. It had not been there when she had left the apartment hours before.

She glared at Ben.

His heterochromatic eyes – one green, the other amber – were open wide. "Let down by Scottie," he said. "I'm surprised you still have that old thing."

"Hush it," she said. She placed Scottie on the table so the rhino would face away from her twin, and hung Van Gogh where he belonged. "This time I reached the Dutch painter and was almost the victor. Will you not give me credit for that?" She pocketed her keys.

"No." He swung his legs to the floor, sat, and crossed his arms, pillow on lap, a fist resting on the side of his mouth. "What you got there?" He pointed to the plastic bag with his pointed chin.

She took the videogame out and smiled. "I have brought endless entertainment for the coming weekend," she said, "and it goes by the name of *Comatose*."

He stood up, placed his pillow under the table, and took the game from her over the table, shaking his head. "You never learn."

"You have appreciated my videogame picks before, Ben.

You were consumed by *The Cauliflower of Doom* for a week and wouldn't let me play it, though it was rightfully mine to enjoy. Then you abducted it and I never saw its pretty little face again. Doesn't *Comatose* sound even better? Don't you want to steal it immediately?"

"No," he said, and handed the game back to her. "It sounds like death," he muttered.

"Certainly, but that means it is ambitious," Alexandra said. She walked around the table, approaching him. "One cannot feasibly create a game around a comatose state."

Ben was not fazed as he munched on a Sweet Tart. "I brought *The Cauliflower* back by the way. Not sure I'm giving it back now. Also, you promised me French toast after the lobster disaster."

"You will not receive sustenance from my hands unless you cleanse yourself," Alexandra said, and sniffed the air. "You reek of yesterday." He only crossed his arms. At the end of the Roman soldier's spear was Ben's bright yellow bath towel rimmed with black. She went to it and felt it between her fingertips – perfectly dry – and looked at her brother with accusation and disgust.

Ben ruffled his bed hair and discreetly sniffed his armpits. He pulled his grey shirt to his face, exposing some of his round belly, and smelled it. "Not my fault I smell of smoke, Alex," Ben said. "You almost set the place on fire."

He was right – the lobster disaster. Ben had been on the couch with a swig of wine when she had somehow set the lobster on fire. Now, she walked away from his scent and into the perfume of burnt lobster. "Benjamin, call me Alex again," Alexandra said, "and no matter how many times you save my kitchen from incineration, the odds of me kicking you out of my house will triple." She opened the fridge door.

She heard him snicker, distant behind the wall. It almost counted as a laugh, and she was grateful for it. "It's an

17

apartment," he said. "Anyhow, when we were kids, you'd only call yourself Alexandra when you were playing queen."

"What if I want to be queen every day?" she asked, smiling to herself. "Besides, you used to call yourself Hector Dragon the Third," she added playfully. She retrieved a small frying pan from the fridge, and in it were a couple of pieces of bread and two white eggs. With the pan, she pushed dirty dishes and a scorched towel to the back of the sink counter.

Ben had poked his head around the kitchen wall, his towel draped around his neck. "I take a shower," he said, pointing with his toothbrush, "you make me food, and then we start playing that weird game?"

"Yes," she smiled wide at him. "And you don't call me Alex."

"I can try."

In a little while, she heard the bathroom door close. She hid the eggs in her skirt pockets and moved her *Lobster Cookbook* from its resting place on her Napoleon bust. "It seems like he has stopped caring for himself for good now..." She let the words ring flat in the lobster-scented air. Alexandra rocked on her feet and counted yoga breaths. "You can do this, Alexandra." She exhaled deep. "Or can you?" she said as an afterthought. She lit the stove burner with a match from the windowsill, picked out a fork from her silverware drawer and put it behind her ear. And thought.

***

Philosophizing under pounding water was not Ben's thing. He was dressed in dark jeans and a T-shirt before Alex had finished. He ruffled his hair in the towel one last time and hung it on the spear end. Then he relaxed on the sofa, smelling good and feeling civilized. He inspected his sister's purchase. The plastic bag urged the user to save the planet in fading green letters. He made room for his legs on the rickety table.

The disc was in a generic CD envelope. It showed through transparent plastic. *COMATOSE* was written in white letters on the disc's black background. The O's looked distinct enough to be someone's handwriting. Ben opened the envelope and let the game slide out onto his palm. A piece of paper tried to follow it out. He pulled at the paper's edge, easing it out of the envelope. Someone must've stuffed it there. It had creases and folds in irregular places. He smoothed the paper on his pant leg. *Microphone required* it said in a scrawl. He slipped his shoes on, sockless. He put the game back into the bag and kept it in his hand. Paper in one pocket and phone in another, he picked up his car keys. His wallet was last, and it went into his back pocket.

"I'm going out," he told the apartment in general. Before Alex could question him, he closed the door. He got into his old, jet-black BMW. With the radio on, he drove the ten minutes to the thrift store.

The inside of the shop was as chaotic as he remembered. He had to get past shelves of aging books to get to the front desk. On the way, he picked up a battered Kurt Vonnegut. Last time he was here, the person manning the desk was an old lady with bottle-bottom glasses. This worker looked like he was having a hard time getting past puberty. He was sure to be hiding a tattoo with his giant analog watch.

"Hey," Ben said to get the clerk's attention.

"Yes?" the boy said, looking up from adjusting his watch. The worker attempted an unflattering smile.

"We bought this earlier," Ben said, and took the game out of the bag.

The worker's pupils widened. "Yes, I remember," he said. "What of it?"

"It says it needs a…" Ben reached into his pocket for the

19

piece of paper. He had to wrestle it away from his keys. "Microphone. You got one for it?"

"Y-yes," the worker said. His face looked like it was about to erupt from embarrassment. "Sorry. I think I have the microphone here." He ducked behind the counter and rummaged through invisible drawers for it.

Ben's smartphone vibrated, and he checked it. It was a message from Alex, asking him where he was. He smiled and put it back into his pocket. When the boy emerged with the microphone, he relapsed to his straight face. "Thank you," he said, taking it from the tremulous grasp. "How much is the book?" The worker opened the book's front cover. Ben looked at the price inside. He paid, rejected a receipt, and strode out of the store. He blasted music on his way back.

Alex was out of the kitchen by the time he walked in. She handed him the plate of French toast and a tomato. She took a slim saltshaker from her pocket and gave it to him. "What was your sudden errand?" she asked, somewhat bitter.

"*Comatose* needs this," he said. He handed her the microphone and bit into the bright-red tomato.

"Oh. You should have inquired about one – I have one. Somewhere."

He wiped juice from his chin before it dripped onto his green shirt. "Well, I didn't. Just use mine, will you?"

Chapter 2

Alexandra sat on her indigo beanbag, flanked by bookshelves, and tried to remember what desk drawer she had stuffed her laptop into this time. She had countless candles and medieval-looking lanterns sitting about her bedroom, one of which was lit to invite a visible yet distraction-less atmosphere. She never opened her curtains or turned the overhead light on in this room, not even to read from her wide assortment of books. It required ambience.

She looked straight ahead at the long desk that took up most of the opposite wall, envisioning their contents rather than seeing the drawers themselves. She closed her eyes and stood up. Her hand reached for the middle drawer. She shook her head and bit her lip, then chose the drawer above.

With a cry of victory, she took out her wireless mouse and laptop. The computer was light and sleek, and certainly quicker than anything Ben would intentionally purchase. She left the room and walked up to the wine couch where Ben sat. She extended her hand, beckoning for the game he held. He was done with his French toast and bit pensively into his tomato.

"I'm still betting failure," he said conclusively, and placed the computer game in her impatient palm.

"Your input is, I am certain, appreciated," she said. She sat cross-legged beside him, and they both watched as her computer whirred to life. She stole a couple of Sweet Tarts and typed in her password.

Alexandra entered *Comatose*. She sensed Ben leaning close, as her salmon background was replaced by a white screen with the word *COMATOSE* written in black at its center. The letters looked the same as on the disc front, but sharper. Before Alexandra could try anything, the screen flicked to black.

"Naturally," Ben said, "I was right."

With a single movement, Alexandra reached across her brother for the microphone and plugged it in. "This battle has not even begun to take shape," she said. "Don't give in on the auction before two parties have accepted to quibble for a price." Before she finished speaking, the white screen returned. From her peripherals, she saw a shadow of a smile on his face. She smirked and pressed the ENTER key.

The title returned for a second only to be replaced with *This is a two-player game.*

"That's exceptionally convenient," she said, and clicked the key again.

The screen went blank. *Your name is Jack,* a sweet, female voice announced.

The game started in third person with the sound of level breathing. The question melted into the small shadow of a man and the world leaked out from him, as if he were a dying black hole. A bright, red sun shone at its peak. Dangerous levels of ever-spreading deep blue quietly overcame the shadow. The man's breathing became louder and labored. The game's viewpoint pushed through his skull and showed his brain, but only for an instant, before it reached his hazel eyes and brought back into view endless deep blue. Now in first person, the screen went black for a second. Then it went back to blue as the man blinked, rudely awakened. His breathing now betrayed a struggle for survival. His two arms, almost indistinguishable through the dark water, floated limp. He was drowning.

"Swim!" Alexandra yelled into the microphone.

The character responded with astounding haste, clawing at the water above him. With labored strokes, he broke the surface. He stopped swimming. The sky brightened as the sun beat down and Jack swallowed gulps of unhindered air, blinking repeatedly. The horizon held only sea, and she took note of the surprisingly good graphics, for an indie computer game.

"Well, that's something," Ben said pitifully.

"Yes," Alexandra uttered. The game's window minimized to half its size, as if shoved aside, and made room for a new window which was nothing but eerie, pulsating, glowing darkness.

"That must be your character," Alexandra said. She moved the mouse tentatively, but she could not discern movement in the second window, and moved Jack's vision instead.

"See, my character's obnoxiously useless," Ben said beside her.

"The operant word is obnoxious, and you haven't even touched the keyboard to prove his uselessness." Alexandra got up and pointed decisively. "My screen is now frustratingly smaller, but that can be easily rectified." She flittered back into her room for an HDMI cable.

***

Ben pressed the arrow keys on Alex's laptop. Jack didn't move, and nothing happened in the blackness. He wouldn't show Alex, but he was interested. Ben's face came closer to the screen. His mismatched eyes studied the black window. He tried to make out a shape or a meaning – anything but pulsating darkness. Nothing. He sighed and put the laptop on the table.

Alex connected the computer to the TV with a long cable, and pulled her game window to the big TV screen. She maximized his window, so it fit the entire laptop monitor. "You have yet to justify your character's existence," she told him, "be it character or black hole." She sat beside him, laptop on both their laps.

"I already tried the arrow keys," Ben said. "I'm out of ideas."

Alex took the mouse. She used it to make Jack look around. His wiry arms glistened in the blinding sun. He shielded his eyes. "Hm…" she said.

Ben slid to the floor with his legs under the table and took the laptop for himself. He tried the arrow keys again. "Nothing," he said. He lifted the laptop up to his sister. Alex was his better when it came to videogames. He never admitted it to his friends.

"I can try W-A-S-D?" she said to herself, taking the laptop. "They're standard keys for a second player." Still nothing. "And you're not the mouse…" she trailed off, thinking.

It appeared only the mouse and microphone did anything. But Alex had given him the useless laptop screen and kept Jack on the TV to herself, so he reached over and tried the arrow keys again, bored. Then, he suddenly stopped.

"What is it?" she asked.

He pointed at the bottom right section of his screen. "I saw something."

"I didn't," she said.

He ignored her, undeterred. "Right there!" He squinted, face and finger almost touching his screen.

Alex laughed. "It isn't doing *anything* different, Ben," she said. "That corner has been glowing all this time."

Ben squinted harder. He was sure he had seen something move. A sort of grey speck.

Then he leaned against the bottom half of the couch. He rested his forearms on it, hands dangling. "I say new game."

He could sense Alexandra's temper rising in indignation. "We are not getting a new game," she said, "we never get a new one whilst playing one, and you should feel ashamed for even mentioning such a thing," she blurted, flustered. She made Jack look around once again with the mouse.

"Can you make him go underwater?" Ben said, and leaned forward.

"Why would I risk such a thing? You saw how he acts underwater. I don't think he particularly enjoys it."

"I want to see how long he can hold his breath."

"I will not."

Ben took the microphone from his sister's unsuspecting fingers. "Go underwater," he said before Alex could stop him.

Jack finally moved again. He lifted his frame as he took a deep breath and went under. "Benjamin!" Alex snatched the microphone back.

Jack tread calmly and rhythmically under the surface. "Aha!" Ben said, attention on the laptop screen.

There was a slow brightness coming from the very center of the dark. A hallway took shape. The lighting stopped at a dark grey. Alex made Jack look around and listened for any change in breathing. There was none. "You can tell him to swim back up when he starts drowning again," Ben said with a dismissive hand. He took the laptop from her and moved with the arrow keys forward down the hall. He instinctively looked around with W-A-S-D. He was always a fast learner.

Jack bobbed underwater until he was out of breath. Ben looked at the TV screen to see the character come up for air and stay afloat without Alex urging him. The image on the laptop screen kept the same shade of murky grey. The hall seemed endless until it stopped at a wall. Ben moved right. The darkness returned to swallow the screen. He backed up and light shone again. He pondered at the corner, looked into the darkness down the new path. He walked forward slowly. The blackness overtook the screen like a mist. He retreated into the light.

"You decide on where to go in your hallway," quipped Alex. "I'm going to follow this fish." She sounded excited.

Ben looked at the TV, then at his sister. "Fish?"

"There is no reason to sound surprised," Alex said. "It's an ocean… although it might be a lake. Either way, fish are bound to appear." She put her tongue out and moved Jack's vision into the ocean. "See it?"

Ben smirked, derisive. "You don't know what you're doing."

"If you would be so kind as to help out rather than belittle, see if you can find anything to do on your screen. I'll focus on giving him directions," she paused. "It might trigger something new on your end."

Ben took a Sweet Tart into his mouth and crossed his arms over each other. "That's not a fish, Alex," Ben said.

***

All I have left are my lungs and willpower, both of which fade fast. The water's ice feels more secure than the sun's burn. The sea is my bed. Soon I will sleep. Soon I will be free.

"Swim!" *she says.*

My eyes focus on the despair ahead of me. I must continue. I mustn't give up. My muscles have regained their lost energy and I swim up with renewed strength. I am alive again.

My name is Jack. I am afloat. My thoughts echo an empty

past.

I loathe the blinding sun with a raw, unspoken hate. It is my enemy. Where am I to go, lost at sea again? Did I arise from the depths for this? I must find a solution quickly. I have tried so many times.

"Go underwater!" *he says.*

The safety of the waters calls to me. I take a deep breath and submerge.

This is where I belong: the water in my hair, the salt stinging my eyes, the wetness one with my skin.

The lack of fresh air is intoxicating.

***

Alex made Jack look into the water again. "If that," she said, "is not a fish, Benjamin, then enlighten me as to what else it could possibly be."

Ben shrugged his shoulders. "Your shadow?"

Alex got up from the couch. She held the microphone, its string taut. "Go underwater," she said.

Jack took another deep breath and submerged. The shape was still there.

"The ocean is far too deep for that to be his shadow," she said. "Swim down."

"It isn't moving," Ben said after Jack went down some more. "Swimming to it does nothing to its shape. Ergo, shadow."

"Stop condemning my inertia and take care of your own," she said in a huff and threw the microphone on the couch. "You have gotten nowhere."

"I have a hallway," Ben said, "and I have darkness. Definitely. You have sea, and a possible fish-shadow."

Alex sat on the floor beside him. Ben sighed deep and moved closer to her. He handed her the microphone still attached to the laptop he held. She sighed.

"Uhm…" said Alex into the microphone. "Reach for the fish-shadow?"

Jack did, slowly. A glow pulsed from the shadow. Then light erupted from it and took over the entire screen. He yelped, surprised, and tried to look away.

A white flash had overtaken the laptop screen. "Woah," Ben said. "Ouch." He blinked the light away. "That's intense."

On the TV, the light took Jack in its arms and lowered him onto a quickly emerging city. His feet hit what looked like a courtyard; his landing lifted dust all around. Buildings made of concrete, brick, and glass could be seen down streets. The computer screen went berserk with pulsating, flashing light. It blinked nonstop. Then it stabilized back into the hallway. The darkness of before scurried away to reveal more hallway that funneled into a tunnel.

Ben looked at the city, then back to his tunnel on the computer. He scratched his chin. "Jackpot," he said.

Chapter 3

"Please," someone said with a whisper mustered into a plea, "not again." Alexandra stared at the television screen and gaped, speechless.

"Was that—" Ben started saying, as surprised as she was.

"Jack?" Alexandra said, microphone close to her parted lips.

"Please," the voice begged.

Alexandra turned and looked at Ben. Her brother's heterochromatic eyes betrayed confusion, and he bit his lower lip. Alexandra hugged herself with an arm, shielding herself from the unknown. "What's the matter?" she asked Jack, tremulous.

"Please not again," the voice replied. "Not again." He shook his head, stumbled forward.

She was afraid he would fall into a heap of despair; all she could do was talk to him. "Again?" she asked. "What don't you want to happen again?" She dreaded an answer, whatever it may be.

"The fire," he said, breathing fast, shallow breaths. "The fire!" He fell to the ground on all fours and stared at the dirt, eyes clouding, chest heaving.

"Breathe, Jack," Alexandra said.

He took a deep breath and exhaled it in a tentative rasp.

"Stand." She sensed fear as Jack looked around slowly but refused to move, like he was unable to do so. Maybe he was paralyzed.

"Is he trembling?" Ben asked.

"It would appear so," she said. "I'm going to try to make him stand... although I feel bad forcing him to do anything." Alexandra got up and sat on the couch, made Jack look up with the mouse.

Jack stood and staggered a step, shaking almost imperceptibly. There was a dried-up, cracked water fountain in front of him. The graphics were incredibly sharp, almost too real for a game. She made him look and walk around the fountain, taking it all in. He seemed to be doing a little better and trembled less. He was in the middle of an old square in a forgotten city with dilapidated buildings all around, some taller than others. Benches that looked too fragile to use framed the square. In the distance, a heat haze lingered over the abandoned streets. Patches of dirt peppered the stone ground beneath his feet. There was no greenery in sight, and everything was covered in bright sunlight and a thin layer of dust, as if a desert had passed through the city and left a little bit of itself behind.

Alexandra completed the full circle and looked over at the laptop with Ben, who was still on the floor. He kept it at arm's length and still looked shocked from the prior flash. He hesitated down the tunnel on his screen and, in no time, reached a dark hallway flanked by bookshelves.

She was distracted from his progress by the TV screen in her peripheral vision. Jack held his head between his hands and closed his eyes. He let out a weak moan and looked ahead, the fountain blurring in his vision. He shook his head to clear it.

"Stop moving," Alexandra told Ben. "You will only distress him more."

"I've had hallway for ages," he said in protest. "Now I have books and you want me to stop? Look at this place!"

The computer screen now was quite a sight. Bookshelves

climbed up the walls as far as the light could reach. The books closer to the bottom were smaller while the ones reaching higher were larger and seemed to span all tones of the color spectrum, though all the books he could see were faded and he therefore couldn't make sense of titles, if there were any. With the dim lighting, the books seemed wedged together, like a confused, faded color spectrum of irregularly-sized rectangles.

"I admire the plethora of books you have at your disposal," she decided, "but you're doing nothing but making him distressed. I am certain we need to explore this ghost town first. Besides," she smirked, "I'm in charge. Therefore, you *will* cease and desist. Until I find out what this new place is." She pushed her hair behind her ears. "Please?" she added.

"Why are you playing as the main character again?" Ben accused her with a glare.

Alexandra smiled sweetly. "Because I'm better at this."

Ben pushed the laptop away on the table, so it was entirely out of his reach. Resigned, he crossed his arms over his chest and sighed. He turned his head to the television screen and reached for a Sweet Tart.

"Thank you, dear brother." Alexandra stuck the tip of her tongue out. She flexed her fingers. "Let's do this, Jack. Walk forward."

***

"Let's do this, Jack," *I hear the enthusiastic voice leap back into existence, plucked from the air around me.* "Walk forward." *I don't understand where it came from, but I don't care. It gives me strength to continue.*

This entire landscape is too familiar – to the point where my

31

blood dries to ice in my veins. The sun overhead is blinding, swathing me in heat. It leaves a bittersweet taste in my mouth, and I have to stop myself from retching. She isn't here, but I feel her presence in the corner of my eyes. When I turn to look, the feeling disappears.

The despair has settled in my stomach, balled into a dull ache. I do not want to remember and start walking out of the square instead.

***

"Now look," said Ben. "My screen went black again."

"Excuse you, brother," said Alex. "Mine is the main screen. Do yourself a favor and keep your eyes on it so you can be of assistance. I want to see how far the horizon reaches."

"Sheesh, touchy," responded Ben. But he knew that tone of voice.

Alex walked Jack out of the square. "Take the mic but keep him walking," she said. "Maybe you can get him talking and find out what troubles him so."

"I make no promises." Ben picked up the microphone. "Jack," he said loudly. He could've sworn Jack jumped. In any case, he halted in his determined stride.

"Yes?" came Jack's voice.

"Fuck," Ben let slip. "This is beyond creepy. He seems too real."

"Benjamin," Alex chided. "I, for one, am enjoying how interactive this game is. Besides, what did you expect would come from bellowing into the mic? He's not deaf, you know."

The last thing Ben had expected to do when he woke was talk about a videogame character as if he were alive. Yet here he was. "Uh… keep walking," Ben told Jack.

Jack started walking again, but his pace slowed.

"Maybe close your eyes so it doesn't feel so 'creepy'?" Alex proposed. Ben breathed a sigh.

"Fine," he said.

"Tell him to stop moving so I can keep an eye on the laptop," Alex said.

Ben gave in and closed his eyes. He gave the order to stop. Then he said, "Do you know where you are?"

"Solstice," Ben heard, Jack's voice filling his head. "I call this hell-hole Solstice." A pause. "I must've been here before. I don't remember."

"Benjamin, it worked!" came Alex's voice. She took the mic from him.

Ben looked at the laptop screen in front of him. The hallway was considerably lighter. Now he could discern where one book ended, and another began. But he saw no titles on the spines. He moved his viewpoint to the right and up, trying to make them out.

"No, no. No…" Jack muttered. He fell to his knees in the middle of the street. The hallway flickered in and out of existence.

Ben sighed deep and lifted himself onto the couch's armrest. "I give up. Just keep on walking, will ya?"

She made Jack walk across a couple more streets and stopped. "I fear that is the fountain in the distance. It can't be."

"Did you manage to walk in circles?"

"I walked straight through and I'm quite sure the main street didn't turn at all. I would've noticed. You didn't see it turn, did you?"

"Not really," Ben said, scratching the beginnings of scruff on his chin. "Yes, that's the same fountain! I remember that crack in it."

Jack was in the square again, and he breathed shallow breaths. "No escape. No escape," he said, putting his hands on the bottom tier of the fountain.

"Sit down, Jack," Alex said into the mic. Jack obeyed and let go of the fountain. He sat down on the dusty stonework in front of it and stared. The details on the fountain sharpened and the crack looked like a gash.

"Solstice must be a very small world," Alex said in wonder. She sat back. "I literally walked its circumference in maybe three minutes."

"Makes it easier to explore," said Ben. He got up. "How about I sit beside you with the laptop?" he said. Alex nodded and he saw her smile. "What?" he said.

"That means you're interested."

"I bet we'll beat it by the end of the day."

"Then we need some bubble tea and cookies," Alex said. Ben looked blankly at her. She jumped off the couch and snatched his car keys. "Come on!"

"You are *not* driving my BMW," Ben said. "Do you even have a license?" He got up.

"I'm not entirely sure!" Alex said. She swiped up her black sneakers and opened her front door. Ben put his shoes on and his phone and wallet in his pockets. He followed as quickly as he could.

***

Ben drove them safely to The Bubble Tea Shop, for he had refused to let Alexandra drive. He said her license might as well be expired since she biked everywhere. He was wrong, but she knew he loved his car, and she didn't feel like driving it anyways; she preferred the leisurely stroll of a bike. She appreciated his driving and was content in the passenger seat, but noticed some candy wrappers and an empty chips bag in the backseat.

"I'll clean it out when we get to the store," he told her, seeing her disapproving gaze while making a turn.

She chuckled. "I said nothing," she said with her hands up in surrender.

"What? Cleaning hasn't been my top priority," he said. His mismatched stare dared her to judge him any further.

She had put on her black sneakers because she knew he would prefer it to neon green, but maybe this time around he wouldn't have cared. It looked like he had forgotten to comb his hair for at least a couple of days. She put on a smile before he noticed her concern. "Well, Sir Benjamin, may I inquire as to what has been of priority?" she asked as innocently as possible.

Ben pondered as he swerved from behind a car that was going too slow. "Survival," he finally said. "Next is that job. Right now, it's just head above water."

"Right," she said. He parked and she got out. "Looks like it's holding up nicely." She stroked the car's side like it was a black cat purring for attention. Ben turned the engine off.

"It's had its ups and downs, but it's been doing okay," he said proudly. "Hasn't failed me since that one fluke."

"I'm glad," she said as he came around the car.

"Good thing I remembered how to get here," Ben said and swung the door to the store open for her.

"Hey, Alex!" the man at the counter greeted her cheerfully. "Ben! Long time no see! Same as usual?"

"Yes," they said unanimously.

"You know y'all always creep me out when you do the twin

thing," he said with a wink.

Alexandra laughed. "Come on, Leon, you know it's not intentional," she said. "Keep the tab open, we're taking some stuff home." She had all the seats to choose from since the store was empty at this time of day. She took the booth and waited for Leon to make their drinks.

Ben didn't follow her. "I thought we were just gonna come in and dash out," he said, looking at her quizzically. She enjoyed telling him only half the plan and, though it irked him, she didn't mind.

"Sit, brother dear," she patted the table in front of her, "and tell me your tales of woe. I am all ears."

"What makes you think I got anything to say?"

Alexandra paused for a moment, then started, "You haven't brushed your hair, I had to make you shower, you didn't want my food last night, you slept on my couch for too long, you've eaten less Sweet Tarts than usual, and you didn't joke with Leon. I know you disapprove of his piercings because you've said they make him look like a skinny elf and yet you didn't mention it. Plus," she added, since she saw he was starting to speak, "you drank some wine before you went to sleep. My favorite one, too."

"It was the first one I found," he objected.

"The wine is the least paramount," she said. To her surprise, he smiled at that, and she chuckled. "We haven't had decent conversation since you came to my apartment. It's all been... shallow banter. I don't like it."

Leon brought Alexandra's mango tea and Ben's almond tea and left them alone to talk. He was good at reading the situation.

Ben picked at his straw pensively but revealed nothing.

"I hate those elusive eyes of yours," Alexandra said. "One looks like a vast forest and the other broad daylight, and yet I can

36

never read them." She might as well drink while she waited, so she sipped on her tea. Ben sat there like a statue, arm on the table, other hand on the drink, lips on the straw but not really moving. He was looking down at his bubble tea like it was going to make her forget everything she had just said and let him drink in peace. But that wasn't going to happen.

"What if I have nothing new to say?" he finally uttered.

"You could say *something*," she said. "I miss having you tell me what's going on. We used to talk all the time, growing up. We're all we've got. That's why you asked to live with me for a time after college graduation, isn't it?"

He said nothing.

"Ben," she said, eyes welling up.

"Sorry. I can't."

"Tricia?" she said the one name neither of them had felt like bringing up.

Ben pushed his drink away toward Alex, staring at the wall behind her. "I'll get the cookies. Chocolate chip?"

"Always," she said, defeated. She sipped more of her drink and walked outside.

The car drive back was silent; the air felt cramped. Benjamin kept his eyes on the road.

Tricia

"Ben, Bobby said Alice is weird." At that time, Tricia was almost three and couldn't say Alex's name right yet. Their parents still used neighborhood playdates as babysitting services when they were working, and the twins were in school. That is where she had met Bobby. They had money to do differently but refused to hire someone. Ben didn't like it. Neither did Alex.

Already nine, Ben knew what bullying was. And Bobby was a bully. Ben stacked up another block and helped his little sister keep it straight. They were kneeling on the dark, hardwood floor.

"Alex isn't weird," Ben said with a wise air. "She's what we adults call 'eccentric.'" He looked over at his twin sister twirling in the garden in the cool summer heat. "Plus, she likes dancing."

"Es…" murmured the little girl. She wore pink shorts and a light blue T-shirt. It was a flash of color in the dark-themed home. She turned her head to Ben, yellow block in hand. "Es—what?"

"Ec-cen-tric."

"I can't say that."

"It's okay."

Alex came back into the house, yellow dress neat, even though she had danced in the sun for about ten minutes.

"Alice," Tricia stopped mid-stacking, "are you ess-en-tic?"

"Who told you that?" Alex asked, hands on hips.

Ben raised his hand.

"Bobby called you weird," said Tricia in an attempt to protect Ben.

"Well, I prefer eccentric," said Ben.

"So do I!" joined in the little girl.

"Well, yes, then Queen Alexandra is eccentric," said Alex. Then she deliberately kicked over the stack of blocks Ben and Tricia (mostly Ben) had painstakingly worked on.

Little Tricia giggled and toppled one over with her finger.

"Why, you…" said Ben.

Tricia squealed and Alex held her hand. "Run!" she told the little girl. Ben chased after them around the expensive furniture. "Wait, not too fast," Alex said. "We don't want to upset mother."

***

Ben set his car keys and tea down on the little table in Alex's apartment. Before she had walked in, he picked up the laptop. "When did you turn the game off?" Both screens were black.

"I didn't," Alex said, "I just paused it by using the ENTER key when you were getting your shoes on. It's the standard for pausing computer games of this kind." She pressed down on the key delicately. "See?" she said. Both screens came back to life. "No progress lost." She set her drink and the cookies down beside his tower of Sweet Tarts.

"Huh," was all Ben could say. "Neat."

Alex got an old notebook from under the little table. She sat down with it on the couch beside Ben, placed the mouse on it. She held the mic in the other hand. "Ready to find out what *Comatose* is all about?" she asked him. He could hear the hope in her voice. So, he said yes.

***

"Did Jack say he lived in Solstice?" Alexandra inquired, trying to make up for the awkward car drive. Ben squinted in thought.

"He called it a hell-hole," he said finally, a fist against his right temple. He picked up his tea. "Would you live in a hell-hole?"

She smiled a big smile. "One never knows what game characters do."

"What are you getting at?" Ben asked, looking at her and sipping at his drink. He seemed more open to conversation after he had noticed she wasn't going to be asking any more questions about their little sister. Alexandra was glad for it.

"Well," she said, biting her lip. "Maybe we can ask him to

39

walk home."

Ben nodded at the microphone in her hand, giving her the cue to try it but not committing to the idea. Alexandra sat back on the couch and breathed in deep.

"Go to your house," she told Jack.

Jack shook his head in confusion. He walked a step around the fountain and stopped. "Maybe he doesn't live in the hellhole," she heard Ben say.

"Maybe he does," she glanced over at him, "but doesn't want to go to it."

"Or maybe," Ben said, voice dripping sarcasm, "he forgot which way home is."

She knew he hadn't intended his suggestion seriously, but she sat in silence, considering it. "He keeps on talking about Solstice like he's been here before," she said. "But he never elaborates."

"Are you saying I'm right?" Ben asked.

"I don't know, brother," she huffed. "I'm taking anything anyone has to offer."

"I offer we walk into a house and figure out what to do in this game."

"That might turn out to be a smart move." She could see Ben smile from her peripherals. That smile was worth trying it out, so she did. "Walk into the first house," she said into the mic.

This time Jack obeyed. He walked slowly yet decisively down a side street toward the house, but did not get close to enter. He said something under his breath and Alexandra couldn't make it out.

"Could you repeat what you said?" Alexandra asked politely.

"No," came Jack's voice. He turned his back to the house, so they saw only dirty street and the square beyond.

Ben chuckled, and she heard him set his cup down. "We got a feisty one."

Alexandra vented her frustrations by dropping the mic and taking her drink. She drank big gulps, swallowing it with the boba and all, not realizing how thirsty she was. She finished her tea and glared at the TV screen.

"Turn around?" Ben asked Jack, tentative.

Jack turned slowly, and the house came back into view. It was small and made of old, red brick that was now covered in a fine layer of gold dust. Dark green curtains covered its four-pane window to discourage anyone from peeking inside. A single streetlamp occupied the sidewalk where the house ended.

Alexandra eyed the screen, skeptical. "Maybe you can make him walk into the house," she muttered, arms crossed.

"Say that again?" said Ben. She looked over at her brother to see him with a small smile.

"You heard what I said, Benjamin." Alexandra slapped him on the shoulder and looked back at the house onscreen.

"Go to the house," Ben told Jack. For a second, the character didn't answer. Then he took one step forward, and another. He came as close as the door and stopped. Alexandra could hear Jack's breathing alter to shallow breaths, but Ben gave it no heed. "Knock," he said. Jack obeyed.

Jack's fist made contact with the wooden door and the scene changed to night, streetlamp on, and the house's red brick color almost could be seen. The lamp illuminated a girl in her twenties standing right inside the door, which was now open, wearing a sweatshirt and sweatpants. She looked cross, frozen in time.

They heard a voice say, *"Are you sure it wasn't normal flirting?"* before the screen altered back to the burning wasteland of Solstice. The girl was gone. The streetlamp went back to

41

looking abandoned, like it had never known how to turn on in the first place.

"No!" Jack said. In a moment, he had fallen to his knees, dust settling around him.

Alexandra could see the computer screen go spastic from the corner of her eye. But she kept her gaze fixed on what Jack was doing. He looked up to the unforgiving sun. "Fire," he murmured, just loud enough to be heard. As if doing his bidding, sunlight overtook what little they could still see of the house, the streetlamp, and everything else. Just as the screen became blinding white, Jack closed his eyes. When he opened them, he was drowning in deep, blue sea.

Chapter 4

"Benjamin, what have you done?" Alex asked. Ben wasn't sure. Alex took the microphone from him. "Swim!" she said into it. Jack kept afloat on the surface of the water.

Ben heard a soft thump come from the computer. He looked at the screen on his lap. A book had fallen off the bookshelf. He looked up at Alex. They shared a confused look. Then his sister smiled.

"Jackpot!" she said. She had stolen his line. She put her fists into the air in triumph, dangerously tugging the microphone. She reminded him of a schoolgirl, with her pleated skirt and wide smile. She reminded him of Tricia. He looked away.

With the arrow keys, Ben walked over to the fallen book. It was dark red. He used W to look up, searching for where the book fell from. He couldn't be certain. He looked back down to the book.

"How do I pick it up?" he asked Alex. But she only shrugged her shoulders. "It's your screen," she said.

"Not fair," Ben said, handing her the laptop. "I helped get Jack to the door."

"Look where that got us," she huffed, still looking at the big screen. Her grip was tight on the microphone. "I let you play as him and you send him back to the ocean."

"But we got a book!" he objected. "Alex…"

"Yes?" she said. She had cocked her nose up at him in disdain.

"Could you please help me out?" he said.

"Certainly, minion," she said cheerfully. Ben shook his head. Alex finally traded the mic for the laptop. She walked over the book. Alex handed him back the laptop and opened her hand to receive the microphone. He handed it over to her absent-mindedly.

The book rose to meet the screen. On its cover was the word *Kat* in gold lettering. It opened. Its pages, beige, as if aged, fit the screen. But they were empty. Ben used the arrow keys to flip over pages until he reached the last one. None of them had writing on them.

Ben took his hands off the keys. "Ugh," he said. "Nada."

"Mm?" Alex asked. She must've been busy because Jack was back on dry land. "Hey!" Ben said. "Stop going on without me."

"Ben, I'm only getting *us* back to where *you* lost us," she said.

"All right, all right, I'm sorry," he said.

"No need," Alex said. But he could see her fight a smile. Ben chuckled. "Attaboy," she said.

"What?"

"You're laughing again," she said, not looking away from the TV screen. Then she looked at him and let her smile loose. "That's my Ben."

Ben smiled the smallest of smiles. "If you say so."

***

Alexandra bit into a chocolate chip cookie. It tasted delicious. The cookie was the first thing she had eaten other than candy since morning. She was so worried about her brother feeling comfortable that she had gone without lunch. It was too late for it now; they were focused. She finished the cookie.

"How 'bout we try another house?" Ben was asking. She looked at him as if he was joking, but he wasn't. "What else are we supposed to do?" he objected.

"You do realize that fire that he cried against earlier," Alexandra said, "is the fire that happens when you get him all upset, don't you?"

"Maybe it's just that house," said Ben.

She pondered over this for a minute, tapping the mic on her knee. "I think," she said, "that I saw a playground when I walked the city." She looked at Ben, who popped a Sweet Tart into his mouth. "Should I try it?"

Ben let out a sigh. "I don't know what to do with this book anyways," he muttered. He had flipped back to its cover. "We need to figure out who Kat is," he continued. "Might as well give it a shot." Ben idly walked down to the end of his aisle of bookshelves, and then back up it, while Alexandra watched, not being able to keep her eyes off his mysterious character, and that's why she noted it first.

"Hold on," she said. "Is that a new hallway?" Ben had almost missed it in his stroll. It jutted out to the left at the beginning of the hallway of endless books, after the hallways that were already there, and seemed to be illuminated by a soft glow. With little hesitation, he walked into it and saw another wall of bookshelves. This one, however, had one dark red book in it that stood out from all the rest, which were, again, faded and dusty. This one was a vibrant color, just at 'arm's length,' and Ben moved toward it and stopped right in front of it. The book fell into his 'hands' (it was still unknown whether his character had hands or not).

Contrary to the *Kat* book they found, this one had no writing on its cover. "Should we keep this for later?" Ben asked.

"I'm not certain you can take it with you," said Alexandra.

Ben tried it: moved back out of the hallway with the book in possession, and once he crossed the threshold, the book flew back, like magic, to its designated place on the bookshelf. "No harm in trying," he said apologetically. "Back to the TV screen and Jack. Do you know whose house that was?"

"I think she's the girl in the flashback," Alexandra explained.

"I was thinking so, too," he said. Ben ran a hand through his hair, and she could tell he was getting a little impatient.

"Should I go to the playground?" Alexandra asked, tentative, glancing at her brother and then at the screen.

"Yes," Ben said.

"Go to the playground," she commanded Jack.

He walked past the street that led to the house they had first gone to, then walked past a side street that looked empty, another with a tall building. Alexandra made him look at them with the mouse as he walked past, but he didn't slow his gait. To his left, she saw one that had lettering on it, and could distinguish a *C*. Later, she would investigate it further.

Jack turned down another side street and was soon at the wooden fence that closed off the playground to the street. It was a plot of land that was just large enough to hold its treehouse, see-saw, monkey bars, and sandbox. Everything looked like it had been abandoned years ago to the fury of time and weather. From where Jack stood, Alexandra could see that the bars looked rusted, the treehouse looked like it was about to fall apart at any moment, the see-saw was stuck in the middle of its journey down, and even the trashcan looked old, dented and battered. All the equipment was covered in a thin layer of dust, just like everything else in Solstice. Alexandra looked at the sign that was pinned by

46

one nail onto the fence. It was lopsided but she could still read it; *No entry after dusk.*

"You could hardly say it's dusk now," she murmured. Ben chuckled beside her. She smiled. "Jack," she said into the microphone.

"Yes?" Jack answered.

"Have you been to this playground before?"

Jack let out what sounded like a short laugh. "Numerous times," he said. Without Alexandra prodding him to, Jack took a step sideways, so he was looking at the playground from an angle.

"Why did you just move?" Alexandra asked.

Jack merely shook his head. "Not now," he said, "please."

"Okay," she acquiesced. "We can talk about that later."

Jack shook his head again but said nothing else.

"It seems locked," Ben said beside her. "How do you enter it?"

He must've said it louder than she thought, because Jack picked up on his voice and immediately put a hand over the fence as leverage and hopped over it. Another scene flashed before them. The lighting was of a sun that had just set. Jack was looking at a girl from a lower angle, like he was sitting down. It was hard to tell by her face – since she was closer to the fence and Jack was beyond the playground equipment – but it looked like the same girl from before, only younger. Alexandra guessed this by her mane of curly hair. In the previous image at the house, her hair had looked longer and well kept, but here it was the same reddish-brown. She wore an oversized T-shirt and was carrying a bottle in each hand.

Words flashed onscreen and Jack read them aloud, but he sounded younger too, "*I stood, hesitant, both hands around my*

Styrofoam cup."

The screen flashed to black then reverted to the Solstice setting. "What was *that?*" Ben blurted out.

Alexandra was looking at the screen intently, daring Jack to stare into the sun and call down the waters once again. He did no such thing but stood, looking at the playground equipment. His vision went blurry, but he blinked once, and it cleared. The playground was still there. She heaved a sigh.

"Look," Ben said, "my character has a fountain pen."

"What?" True enough, there was a fountain pen on the computer screen.

"One of those fancy pens that need inkbottles," Ben replied.

"I know what fountain pens are, brother dear, I want to know why you have it." She shifted, uneasy, on the sofa.

"Maybe to write the title on a book that's in this other new hallway of books that I found?" Alexandra looked up, and Ben was shrugging. He was looking at the computer screen, waiting for her to catch up.

He meant the next hallway after the first one where they had found a red book. Ben made his character walk in and, sure enough, there were two shiny, new, red books that needed help with a title. He hovered up to one of them and 'walked' closer to it. It came down from its perch on the bookshelf spine forward, oscillating slightly, as if waiting impatiently. Ben used the keyboard keys to write in *Playground.* He put the book back silently. The fountain pen opened the menu and slotted itself beside the *Kat* book, which was tucked away, smaller, in the corner of the screen.

***

This place holds so many jarringly different memories. A simple playground, yet it became so much more. It became her, *young and innocent. It became me, young and hopeful. It now held both of us in its clutches and won't let go.*

"Jack?" *asks the female voice of before.*

"Yes?" I reply. I don't know who this person is, but she has been guiding me. She has kept me going. Maybe I will have the chance to thank her someday.

"Have you been to this playground before?" *she inquires. Her voice holds curiosity. How am I not to answer? Maybe answering will help her get me through this.*

"Numerous times," I say, and chuckle.

I think of the last time I was here. Here, at this very fence, in this very spot. I move away.

"Why did you just move?" *she asks.*

"Not now. Please." I shake my head to clear it from the memory that wants to claw its way into my heart and reach my very core.

"Okay," *she says.* "We can talk about it later."

I hope to God she forgets and doesn't bring it up at a later time. But I know she won't let it go so easily. I have acted oddly, and she has caught me in the act. She is a cunning one.

I hear the male voice, almost a whisper. "How do you enter it?" *he asks. So, I show them how I did it a number of times before, even before I met* her. *Like a piece of paper that has jammed itself into a notebook, I can't shake her free. Perhaps I need to learn to stop trying.*

***

"How do you reach your books?" Alex asked Ben.

"I don't know. I sort of… hover over to them with W," Ben replied, common-fact.

"Your character isn't a person," Alex explained, "so maybe it's an entity. It would make sense that it could hover. But how, then, would they hold the fountain pen, with no hands or feet, for that matter?" She tilted her head with the question.

"Magic," said he. "All magic."

"Hmph," she half-sighed, defeated.

Ben picked the book he had christened *Playground*. Pressing UP again, he opened it. But he was face-to-face with blank pages. He put the book back.

Ben sighed. This game was going to be tough. "Maybe the pages will fill out as we go along?" he asked Alex.

His sister bit her lower lip in thought. "With the scenes?"

"Yeah," Ben said.

"To be fair," said Alex, "it does sound like a story." Ben sipped at the last of his bubble tea.

"Not so much failure as you thought it was, is it, Benjamin?" Alex asked. He looked at her. She had her smirk on. Ben sighed.

"I'll admit it," he breathed out. "You were right."

"Thank you," she said. "I'm starving," she continued as an afterthought.

"You didn't eat?"

"The chocolate chip cookie and some Sweet Tarts," Alex said defensively, pitifully. Ben made his mouth into a comical O.

"Shame on you!" he said. "Go make yourself some toast."

"Okay, okay," she muttered. Alex got up and headed to the kitchen. She looked back at him. "Don't make him drown again," she warned.

With a hand, Ben zipped his mouth shut and threw away the key. Alex smiled big. She continued on her way.

She was finally out of sight. Ben sat on the sofa, legs crossed, and leaned forward so he could squint at the bookshelves before him. There was no sense to them. He knew now that he didn't need to worry about the other colored books, for he couldn't write on their spines. He was just happy that he found another hallway to walk down.

He had a second thought. Maybe his character's objective was to fill out the book. He tried picking up the book and typing again. He typed *Hesitant, Styrofoam* cup into the pages of the book. Maybe Jack would approve.

Ben caught himself. Since when did he start thinking Jack was a real person, in a place of authority? Perhaps since he had said 'no' to Alex. His sister had acted upset. A non-compliant videogame character making Alex disgruntled? He smiled at the thought.

The three words he put in parted, and made way for the sentence, *I stood, hesitant, both hands around my Styrofoam cup*, to be written on the lines of the book.

Ben instinctively looked up to the TV screen. Jack gave him a nod and remained calm. Ben let out a taut breath. He hadn't messed up. Putting anything into the first red book, however, might be dangerous. He put away the thought and pressed the ENTER key.

***

Alexandra returned to the living room with two bowls of mac and cheese. She held one fork in her mouth with her teeth and had another in the bowl intended for Ben. Both screens were black – her brother learned quickly. Maybe he had grown tired of the game or maybe it had drained him; she couldn't tell. He had placed her laptop on the rickety table and now had his own resting on his crossed legs.

She noticed, for the first time all day, that Ben looked weary. He most likely was searching for jobs online, like he had been the night before. But she imagined he wasn't really looking. From his fixed gaze, it looked like he was scrolling, not really taking any of it in. She sighed and he looked up in response.

"Food!" he cheered, and she managed a smile at his enthusiasm. "Isn't it a bit early?" he said.

"You told me to eat," she said around her fork, moving in front of him to sit on the sofa, "so, I kind of decided to call it dinner."

Ben smirked and took the bowl of food. Mac and cheese was one of their shared favorite dishes. She took the fork out of her mouth.

"What is it today?" Alexandra asked. "Indeed or Monster?" She glanced at his laptop screen and saw he was on *indeed.com*.

"Both," he said, switching tabs to show her.

"How many have you applied for?" She hadn't asked this last night and she was afraid of what the answer might be.

"Don't ask hard questions," he said.

Alexandra looked down at her Mac and Cheese, picking at it with her fork. She knew she wouldn't get much else out of him, so she changed topics. "Did you get bored of *Comatose*?"

"Oh, I need to show you something." Ben reached over and clicked ENTER on her waiting laptop. He pointed at the screen, almost touching it. "Look what I did," he said with pride. She read the narration on the page, then looked over at Jack's screen.

"Was it in the book like we thought?" she said, eager. Maybe they were getting the hang of this game after all.

"Nope," said Ben with that same pride in his voice. "I had to type them in myself."

"And Jack didn't flinch?" she asked, surprised.

"Nope," he replied, decisive. "But oddly enough, he nodded," he added posthaste.

Alexandra looked at the book again and read the words on the page. "You remembered all of it?" she asked.

"No," Ben said, and set his fork back into his food. "I put in the key words and the rest filled itself out."

Alexandra finally remembered her own food and took a forkful into her mouth. She had forgotten, once again, that she was hungry. Who could blame her? This game was becoming more interesting by the second. She pressed the ENTER key.

"And you said he nodded?" She looked up to the black screen, as if it would reveal its secrets to her.

"Yeah, like he knew I was doing it right. I'm telling you, Alex, this game is creepy."

"What do you think the hallways and bookshelves are?" she pondered aloud. The yellow, cheesy goodness of the mac and cheese was inviting her to take another bite, but she ignored it. "Maybe he's looking for a book and can't find the right one?"

"No," said Alexandra, "that wouldn't explain his visceral reaction to that first house."

"Maybe he's traumatized?" she heard Ben question in a near whisper.

"Clearly," she huffed. "He's traumatized by the city he is in. Wait," she said, fork in the air, "you mean by the story?"

"Yeah, maybe it's his story." Ben put his bowl down on the table in front of him. "His life."

"That would explain the first-person point of view." All the gears were finally clicking into place in Alexandra's head. She tapped the fork against her teeth in thought. "It still doesn't explain his reaction to the house."

"Maybe…" Ben started.

"They're memories!" they both said at once.

"That would explain his reaction to that first image we saw!" said Alexandra, excited.

"So, the hallways of books… are his memory library?" Her brother looked as thoughtful as she had felt a second ago.

"Yeah, literally!" she said. "Wow."

"Wow," he repeated. They exchanged a glance. "You picked a good videogame," Ben finally said.

"Yes, I did," she said, but she was hardly paying attention. The wheels in her head were already spinning.

"Again," she heard Ben say, his voice making its way through the recesses of her working mind.

***

Ben looked at his sister. He picked his bowl back up and got a forkful of mac and cheese.

It had bacon bits in it, just how he liked it. He knew by the blank look on Alex's face that his sister was currently lost to him. Though he wasn't that hungry, he might forget to eat later. So, he ate and finished his bowl quickly. He set it down and it made a sound. It was jarring enough to wake Alex from her thinking. He almost apologized. But she looked happy to be out of her daydream.

"I know what," she said. "Maybe…" So she hadn't been done thinking.

"Take your time," said Ben. The blank look came back, but only for a couple of seconds.

Then she was awake to the world again.

"Maybe we have to piece the memories together…" she said, thoughtful.

"Yes," Ben agreed.

"And then we can get along to later memories," she said. "I could tell this was a puzzle game the minute we didn't get directions on how to play."

"That's because you bought the game at a thrift store. It had no instructions with it."

"Even so, Benjamin," she patronized, "the game itself would've told us how to play. At least given us the first clue as to what needed to be done. But this game has left us in the dark from the beginning. Sometimes quite literally." She put food into her mouth.

"Do you think that's why he had a visceral reaction to the brick house? Because it wasn't in the right order?" It was Ben's turn to put a blank, thinking face on.

"Possibly," said Alex. "Perhaps that is the case, but it was also too violent a response to be just that. The sun came down and the game restarted."

"But it gave us the *Kat* book," he objected. He still felt guilty for the restart.

"That only means we are in the right direction," she said. "And if we are in the right direction…" She pointed at her laptop screen with her fork.

"We need to keep on collecting pieces of memories," he finished for her.

"Precisely," said Alex with finality.

"Should I get the book for that first scene?" he pondered, grasping at straws.

"I imagine he wouldn't be ready to let you write in it," she said. She put her fork into her mac and cheese. Twirled it around, still more focused on thought than food.

"Good," he said with a smile, "'cos I don't remember what it said."

"Something about flirting."

"That wouldn't be enough," he said. He threw his head back on the sofa. "There was more to it."

Alex munched thoughtfully. She looked at him with a disapproving glare. It soon subsided. "Sadly, I was too taken aback to remember much else of it," she muttered.

"Obviously, that was her house," Ben said. He looked at the blank TV screen. "We know that much."

"Truly?" his sister asked.

"She was wearing sweats!" Ben pointed out. "What other house would she be in?"

"I like to keep my mind open, remember?" Alex poked her temple with a finger from her free hand. "It is never useful to simply jump to conclusions. Easy, but never useful."

"Anyhow," he said, ignoring her, "it sounded like she was rejecting him." He internally winced at the thought. Poor Jack. Rejection was never kind.

"We don't have enough to tell that was the case," she looked into his eyes with her amber ones, urging him to discuss the idea with her. She always liked to see sparks fly. He wasn't going to take the bait. It wasn't worth the argument.

"Trust me," he said.

"You have prior experience?" she rebutted, ever prodding.

"Alexandra, I'm a grown man. Of course I've been rejected before." Ben picked up his bowl and stood.

"You don't act like a grown man," she smirked.

"I'm about to put my bowl into the sink," he said. "Grown enough?"

Alex stuck her tongue out at him. "Only if you wash it, too."

Ben shook his head, but he could feel a smile creeping in.

She always had something to say back. He walked toward the kitchen to move away from her prying gaze.

"Could you get me a glass of water?" she asked him from the other room.

"Sure," he called back.

As soon as Ben entered the kitchen, he was stunned by the smell of burnt lobster. It would probably be a while before the scent left.

Ben put his bowl into the sink. She had left the pan of Mac and Cheese to soak in the sink. He looked around the room, and had to smile. This kitchen was clearly marked as Alex's. He saw an eclectic assortment of bowls and plates in cabinets above the sink. Ben would be surprised if he ever found something that matched. Napoleon's bust was something his sister must've acquired in the same thrift store where she had found *Comatose*. It had a yellow cap on its head. By the stove was an array of spices in little glass bottles on a wooden shelf. He found the wooden spoon she had used to stir the meal with right below the spices. Ben put it in the sink.

If she hadn't cleaned up after herself, neither would he. They had a game to play. He walked back to the living room in time to see Alex pick up her now empty bowl. She squinted at him. He sat back down.

"You didn't wash your things, did you?" she said.

"I took your lead and left it to soak," he replied.

"You forgot my water, too," she accused.

"Knew I was forgetting something." Ben sighed and made to get up.

"I'll get it," she said, already leaping off the couch.

"What next?" he said, loud enough for her to hear him from the other room.

"I think I saw a café," she said, barely audible.

Chapter 5

Alexandra caught herself thinking about her brother while she filled two glasses with water from the jug in her fridge. She was extremely happy that Ben was starting to act a little more like normal, but she tried to refrain from showing it. Maybe he would clam back up into being morose if he himself realized that he was allowing himself to appreciate life again. Over the past four years, Ben had spent all his energy on becoming a chemical engineer, even when she had called him to catch up when he was in college. But now he hardly put effort into finding a job in his field. She noticed that he was shooting in the dark, even looking up dishwashing jobs, like he wasn't sure of what he should be doing. She was trying to help him get well again, but that was hardly going to happen if he refused to talk to her. Maybe he needed to help himself. At this point, she wasn't sure.

She sighed and headed back into the living room, where her brother still sat, pressing arrow keys. She offered him the bigger cup and he took it. In one gulp, he had downed half of his water while she sipped at hers. Ben looked at her.

"You'll die of dehydration if you drink your water like that," he told her. Alexandra gave him a glare and took a big gulp. "Better?" she asked.

"Certainly, Alexandra," he said. His voice was cheerful, and so were his mismatched eyes. Alexandra smiled back at them and sat back beside him, taking the microphone and mouse so she wouldn't sit on them. She noticed he had gone back to pressing keys.

Alexandra looked at the laptop screen and saw Ben was walking aimlessly up and down a hallway. He was waiting on her.

"Café?" he asked, not looking up. He must've noticed her gaze on him. She let the thoughts of his behavior slip away into the back of her mind and put the microphone close to her mouth.

"Walk to the café," she said into it. Surprisingly, Jack didn't move. Maybe he didn't know where it was or, maybe, as Ben would've pointed out to her, he didn't want to go to it. Alexandra guided Jack down the street where she had seen the building with the letter *C* on its front. The entirety of the letters said *Tom's Café*. It looked completely abandoned, and the lines on the concrete to indicate parking spots were faded, almost non-existent. But she noticed something strange about its side: it was missing a piece, like a wrecking ball had eaten into it.

"Walk in through the hole in the wall," she told Jack. The more she commanded him, the easier it was to do and the less strange it felt. Jack obeyed, stepping over rubble. He stopped so she could look around, and so they could all see what was inside *Tom's Café*. It looked different from any café she had ever gone to.

"Did it always look like this?" Alexandra asked Jack.

"No," he answered. "It was always busy," he finished.

It looked busy now, but full of things, not people. There was a counter that fringed all of its remaining walls, except the front desk, and it was covered with an assortment of objects.

There were four round tables in the open space and those, too, were cluttered with objects that looked completely random. Some of it had spilled to the floor, and it was half-covered in miscellaneous objects as well. It reminded Alexandra of a dump site. There was anything from a doll's head, to dumbbells, to white roses, to wooden toy cars, to necklaces, to a cathode ray TV, to a piece of art. Everything was covered with an extra layer of dirt. She imagined this place was here for them to look for objects that would help them recover memories, but had a hard time looking for a Styrofoam cup in the middle of all the mess, even though the objects were crisp and easy to discern, due to the excellent graphics of *Comatose*.

"Find a Styrofoam cup?" she asked Jack, not sure if it would work. Ben had caught onto her plan, for he didn't object to her order just yet.

Jack picked his way among the motley of objects, looking around as he went. He ignored much of it, but some of it he took a closer look at before moving away. It was a lot to keep up with, and Alexandra gave up trying to, thinking to herself that she would have time to search this place properly at a later time. But Ben thought differently.

"You're letting him do all your hard work!" Ben exclaimed beside her.

"The game allows it, so it's not wrong," Alexandra pouted, looking at her brother. He had crossed his arms again. "Who knows? Maybe it will help him remember some other things." She gave him one last hopeful look before turning her attention back to the TV screen, where Jack was still searching. He passed by a canvas that was covered in red paint but hardly gave it a passing glance.

"You don't know what you're doing, do you?" Ben asked.

"I didn't say that," she replied, not breaking eye contact from Jack's search. But Ben might as well be right.

"You don't," he prodded.

"I don't," she finally admitted.

Just then, Jack spotted what looked like a dented Styrofoam cup. Alexandra stared intently at the TV screen, and she was sure her brother was doing the same. She wanted to know if Jack would pick the Styrofoam cup up voluntarily. He touched it, and an image flashed on the screen.

Jack was looking up at a sky full of stars. He narrated the words that appeared on the screen: *I could hear her place the empty bottle by the full one and she lay down, beer and glass the only thing between us.*

The image of stars faded away and the dust-covered innards of the café were back. Jack now held the cup in one hand.

"Don't tell me," Ben said, and Alexandra looked at him quizzically. "We need to find a bar," he murmured.

"Maybe we do," she said, and looked back at the dusty café.

"Permission to put that line of narration into a book?" Ben asked. "Before we forget it," he added. She looked over at him, and saw he was already on the move and was in the hallway with the two red books, one already entitled *Playground.* He opened the second, nameless red book and was about to type in it.

***

"No," she objected. She pressed the ENTER key and halted the game.

"What?" Ben asked. He looked at his sister. Alex had a look of concern on her face. "I don't think that's where it goes," she explained.

"Why not?"

"Because…" she started, "it doesn't feel right."

He put his hands flat on the keyboard. "I need more than that," he said. Alex put on her thinking face. He waited. She finally spoke.

"Jack touched the Styrofoam cup and the memory emerged," she said, enumerating her thoughts on her fingers. She looked at them.

"And…?" Ben said, crossing his arms over his chest.

"That means the memory is related to the Styrofoam cup snippet," Alex explained, gaze on him quickly, then back at her fingers. "Kat has two beer bottles with her when Jack sees her in the playground," she said, shifting in her seat, finally fixing her look on his eyes.

"We only saw them from far away," Ben said, growing impatient.

"I'm quite certain that is what they are," she said quickly, so she didn't lose her train of thought. "And if that's the case, it's the same memory as the one where we see her from afar in the playground. Jack still sounded as young when he narrated this memory as he did when he narrated that playground memory."

"I didn't notice," he said, unwavering, examining a swirl in the hardwood floor.

"He did. I swear he did," she pleaded, putting her hands on her skirt.

"Even if you're right, he might be the same age when they're somewhere else involving beer and Styrofoam cups." He locked eyes with her.

"You think closer to the entrance of the hallway means young?" she said, inquisitive.

"Why not?" he put lamely.

"All right. Now, I gave you my arguments, you give me yours."

"The game wouldn't give us more than one piece for each memory," Ben explained.

"We agreed that we had to put snippets of memory together to access a memory," she said. Now she was the one growing impatient.

"But we hadn't counted on finding the cup to conclude that memory," he continued, undeterred.

"I would much rather find that out before assuming it to be the case," Alex said.

"Why did you go to the coffee shop in the first place?" he asked, changing the subject entirely.

Ben looked at her with earnest, challenging her.

"I had a hunch, and I was right," she said simply.

"We also hunched that finding what we needed for one memory would set off a new one," he said, crossing his arms again. His gaze fixed on the swirl.

"That isn't how I meant it, Ben," she said.

He looked at her. She had a frown on. "And now we have what might be a new memory! It might be one for the second red book!" Ben threw his arms up in indignation.

"I have played complicated games, and *Comatose* seems like one of them. Finding a second memory this quickly doesn't sit well with me," she said, resolute. Neither of them were about to budge.

"Maybe," he said in exasperation, "the game is easier than you give it credit."

Alex sighed and pressed the ENTER key again. The game came back to life. "Do your worst," she mumbled. Ben barely heard it. He typed in *Beer and glass between us* into the first page of the book.

Instead of the word-filling that he expected, the words were shaken loose from the page. The book snapped shut and fell to the ground. Ben looked at Jack's screen. He was shaking his head vigorously. Blinding white made its way into his line of sight and engulfed it. The screen went black for a split second. Then it was a sea of blue.

"Dammit," Ben said. He looked back at the laptop screen; he had been brought back to the first, empty hallway. Beside him, Alex was already telling Jack to swim to Solstice. With haste, Ben walked down the hallway to the *Kat* book on the floor. He assumed it slotted itself away in the menu screen when it disappeared from his view. Then he found the *Playground* book in its hallway, on its bookshelf and opened it. All its pages had gone blank. "Dammit," he said again.

***

Alexandra thought of telling Ben that she had told him so, but decided against it. She was bewildered as to why he hadn't trusted her instincts and experience. Having pondered on it, the only explanation she could find was that Ben had learned to trust himself and no one else. She was hurt that this had extended to her, but wasn't about to bring it up. He looked dejected already, slumped forward, hands limp on the keyboard, mismatched stare on the empty virtual book open before him.

She had managed to put Jack back on dusty, dry land in one command: "Swim to Solstice." She was surprised it had worked.

"Did we lose the cup, too?" Ben asked in a crestfallen voice. Alexandra looked at him – he still stared at the laptop screen.

"Yes, but no need to worry, I'll go straight back to the café and find it." Ben said nothing.

"Hey," she said, putting a hand on Ben's shoulder. He finally looked at her. "Do you remember the keywords for the two snippets?"

"Yeah," he said.

"Put them into the book you named *Playground* before I get to the place and have nothing to work with." Alexandra smiled, and she hoped it helped. Determined, Ben started typing, which made her smile bigger.

"I should learn to trust you more often," Ben said, voice low. Alexandra had to stop herself from saying 'You used to.'

"It's okay," she said. "Walk down the street to your left," she told Jack.

She guided him into the café and told him to find the cup, which he did, this time with ease. Maybe all was not lost to the blinding white sun. He grabbed the cup, but the scene and narration did not happen. She looked over at Ben and the laptop: he was looking at the TV screen, book already in its place back on the shelf. Perhaps the scene no longer showed when the snippet was set in place into the right book. She chuckled, and Ben looked pleased.

"Ben," Alexandra said, and her brother turned his head to look at her.

"Yes?"

"Would you like to do the honors?"

"Whatever you say goes," he said, and put his hand out for the microphone. He sounded eager, which made her happy.

They had no need to be having a heated discussion like they just had, and she decided that after they recovered the *Playground* memory, they would stop playing for the day. *Comatose* was draining them.

Ben directed Jack to the playground and had him enter it. "Do I just... sit on the dead grass?"

"I believe so."

"Sit on the dead grass," he said with determination. "Facing the playground," he added for good measure.

Jack did as he was told and sat. He looked up at the blinding sky and it flickered into growing darkness. When he looked down, Jack was outside the playground again, sipping at the cup he still held.

"Look," Ben said. Her brother was looking at the laptop screen, so she looked at it, too. The *Kat* book had opened before them, and its pages were suddenly filled with narration. Jack's voice, young, read it aloud as the scene played out before them.

***

Penumbra overtook the playground. I jumped over the fence with my vanilla latte and sat on the grass beyond the playing equipment. Everything was peaceful. Plastic pails and rakes were left behind in the sandbox by a wayward child. One swing, lazy, lifted in the slight breeze. The quiet gave me time and space to think. Legs extended on the grass, sipping at my drink; I looked up at the stars peeping through the rapidly darkening sky and wondered at humanity's insignificance.

I heard footsteps, soft, crunching the gravel ahead of me. No one was allowed in the playground after dusk. Someone had trespassed the grounds, just as I had. I put my head back down to get a look of the intruder.

A girl about my age, sixteen, walked toward me with a bottle in each hand. Her hair was curly and wild; it looked like a chestnut-colored mane around her face. She wore an oversized T-shirt, blue jeans and sneakers. As she came closer, I could tell she held two beer bottles. Soon I could make out her face. Her slender nose was a contrast to her big, dark-brown eyes. Her chin was strong-willed and determined. I stood, hesitant, both hands around my Styrofoam cup. She was looking at me with furrowed brow, eyebrows delicate.

"Hi," I ventured. "I'm Jack." I was about to extend a hand to her in greeting but remembered hers were otherwise occupied. She smiled wide at my mistake, a single dimple on her right cheek.

"Kat," she curtsied, still looking at me quizzically. The name came out in one small breath, like she was uncertain whether I was safe to talk to. She made up her mind and offered me a beer. "My friend bailed on me," she explained. Her voice was melodic. "I stole these from my dad's collection," she added as an afterthought.

"I'm more about coffee," I told her as an excuse. I raised my cup. She clinked her other beer, open and a quarter empty, against my drink. It made no sound, but she was satisfied. She took a swig then clicked her tongue.

"Bitter," she winced. "Oh well, hope it gets better." She took another big gulp, and this time didn't make a face.

"Want some of my latte?" I asked. She didn't run away at the awkward question, which was a good sign.

"Nah," she replied, "I'm set." She placed the bottle she hadn't opened on the grass. "It's here when you want it." It toppled over on the uneven terrain, but she didn't move to pick it up. "What is it, weirdo?" she asked and sat down. I hadn't noticed I had been staring. She glared up at me, defiant.

"Sorry." I shook my head. I wanted to tell her she was beautiful but couldn't form the words. "I've never seen you around." I was uncertain of what to do with myself, so I sipped at my latte. "May I?" I asked, gesturing at the other side of the bottle, where I had been sitting.

"Sure," she said. She moved the unopen bottle closer to

herself to make room for me. "First time I come here after dark," she shrugged. "Looks a lot different than it does in the afternoon." She picked at a blade of grass and sighed. "Same old playground, though."

I wanted to ask her what brought her here, if she had younger siblings that she took to the playground in daylight, and if she planned on drinking both beers now that I had declined mine. But all I could think to say was, "I come here for the silence."

Kat nodded. "I came here to escape my dad." She took a swig. "He's a mean drunk."

"Is that why you took his drinks?" I interjected.

"Nope," she said, and drank some more. "Just wanna know what type of drunk I am." I took a lukewarm sip of the little coffee I had left.

"Found out yet?" I inquired.

"I think," she replied, raising a slender finger, "that I'm a happy drunk." She smiled that wide dimpled smile. "Now, what are you?"

"I never wondered enough to find out," I answered. I didn't want her to know that I had never had a drink before.

She looked at me up and down, sizing me up. "Hm..." she uttered. "I bet you're a talkative drunk," she concluded and went back to her blade of grass. "We usually become what we don't let ourselves be when sober."

I drank some of my coffee in silence and thought on all she had said. "I believe in restraint," was what I could come up with.

"You do?" she asked. She turned her body so she could face me. "Why?"

"Because there's a thing called dignity."

"Dignity only gets you so far in life," Kat smirked. "You

gotta live a little!"

"Why don't you let yourself be happy, then?" I objected.

"Hm?" Her bottle was nearing empty.

"You said we become what we aren't," I explained, "and you become happy."

"Oh," she said. She placed her bottle on the ground and held it by its neck. "You believe in dignity," she rebutted, "but you're here, trespassing just like me."

I smiled at her counterargument and drank the last of my latte. "This is different," I said.

"You could still get caught."

"So could you." I threw my empty cup down. "This is worth it." I laid down in the grass, felt it prick at my skin. "No one can see you from the street when you're in this deep."

"I did," Kat replied. I could hear triumph in her voice. I turned my head to look up at her. "Cars, I mean."

"Specifically cop cars?" She emptied the last of her bottle into the grass.

"Yup." I looked back up at the stars. I could hear her place the empty bottle by the full one and she laid down, beer and glass the only thing between us. I could smell the faintest scent of cinnamon coming through the overpowering smell of drink. I tried to keep conversation going. "Have you told your dad you don't like it when he drinks?"

"Pfft," she scoffed. "He doesn't listen to me. I tried to convince Mom to ask him to stop, but she thinks it's just a phase." She pushed the bottles, so they clinked against each other. "It's been a phase for years now," Kat concluded. Her voice betrayed sadness.

"I had an uncle," I said. "Drunkard, too."

"Had?"

"His liver called it quits."

She laughed, and that was melodic, too. Kat seemed like someone I didn't want to lose sight of. I wanted to spend the rest of the night in the grass with this beautiful, mysterious girl, but I had homework left. "Want to meet up at the coffee shop tomorrow?" I asked, surprising myself. "I can get you a hot cocoa if you're not the coffee type." I looked at her out of the corner of my eye. She sat up and crossed her arms.

"Why would you want to do that?" she spat. The question caught me off guard. I sat up, too, palms down on the grass behind my back.

"So you don't bring contraband beer?" I chuckled.

"No. Why would you want to see me again?"

This question caught me even more off guard than the first. Because you're pretty and I just developed a crush on you? Because you seem like you need a friend that won't bail on you? Because I want to make sure you're safe and don't open that second bottle and get a hangover? "Because I think you're cool," I said, standing up.

"Ah. You gotta leave," she said, more statement than question.

"Yeaaaah... homework."

"So you're the scholar, huh," she concluded. "Figures. The latte should've told me." She picked up both bottles and got up, nimble. She stretched, waving them in the air as she did so. "I got homework, too," she said. "I guess."

"See you at dusk?" I asked, and bent down to pick up my cup.

"Okay," she said. She skipped to the trashcan and threw both beer bottles into it. I sighed relief and hoped she didn't hear. "You bring me a caramel latte – no whipped cream – and I'll be

here, in the playground," she said. She turned around and saw my look of confusion. "Coffee shops are crowded," she explained.

I walked over to where she stood and threw my cup in the trashcan. She extended her hand.

"Nice to meet you, Jack," she said. Her smile was timid, but the dimple was there.

"Nice to meet you, Kat," I replied, and shook her hand firmly. It was cold from the beers. I jumped over the fence, and she followed suit. Suddenly, we could see headlights approach in the distance. She gave me one last laugh and ran down the sidewalk in the direction I presumed was home. I ran, too, but in the opposite direction toward mine. I smiled at myself. Had I just asked out a girl I had just met? Had she just said yes?

***

With the narration over, Jack took another step away from the playground and stepped on a piece of bright light on the sidewalk. The light rose up around him and reached his eyes, making him blink. With the second blink, he was back at Solstice, sun and dust touching everything. Jack shook his head, confused, and did not move.

"Huh," Alexandra heard Ben say beside her. "Neat."

"That was amazing!" she said, and looking at her brother confirmed it: there was a smile on his face. She reached over his hands, still poised over the laptop, and clicked the ENTER key.

"What was that for?" he asked. She patted his hand.

"Hands off," she said, "that's it for today." Ben obeyed reluctantly.

"But it just got good! We just unlocked a memory!" he

protested as she picked the laptop up from his lap. Alexandra stood up and looked her brother straight in his indignant eyes.

"We just argued over this game just a few minutes ago. That means we need to call it quits." Ben sighed at her remark. "Remember?" she asked with a plea in her voice. This wasn't the first time a game had gotten between them, and this time it had happened quicker than she had expected. "We need a break," she concluded.

As response, Ben reached into the bag from the thrift store and took out a book by Kurt Vonnegut. She had seen the lump in the bag, assumed it was a new book, and was happy to see she was right. He started reading without giving her a second glance. She put her smile away, detached the microphone and HDMI, put them beside his car keys, picked up the wireless mouse, and the laptop, and walked the short distance into her room.

Alexandra sat at her desk, pensive. She still hadn't found the time to figure how to quit *Comatose*. She un-paused it and pressed keys until the game offered her the solution. It was the SHIFT button, which made both screens, which were now back on the laptop, fade over. On the hallway screen, the words SAVE AND QUIT appeared in bold white letters. She clicked ENTER, and the game disappeared from her screen.

She opened Chrome and meditated on *Comatose*, her fingers hesitant over the keys of her laptop's pristine keyboard. Her thoughts were mostly scattered, somewhat excited, about the game that she had picked by the guidance from a customer at the thrift store – the game that showed itself to be more than she could have imagined it to be. She was always pleased when she found just what she needed for the day, and since Ben was being more aloof that he had been the last time she had seen him, just a week ago at his college graduation, what she had needed was something for them to be excited about together.

Putting that thought aside and against her general practice, Alexandra opened Wikipedia and searched for *Comatose, game*. To her surprise, she found nothing to assist her. She didn't recollect having seen the game's creator displayed when they had first opened it, and she opened it again and made sure that it was lacking. This was rather odd. She had guessed that the game had been made by some unknown indie company, and for that very reason she was astounded that they hadn't tried to at least make themselves known.

She changed tactics and searched for the game on Google; message boards, articles, etc. Infuriatingly, she kept coming up with medical articles and other such sites. Certainly, none of them were of use to her, not even at giving insight about why the game creators had given it such a name. She narrowed the search down to *Comatose game Solstice* and still came up with nothing. Curious, she tried *Comatose game microphone* and finally found something. She shot a fist up into the air in triumph as she opened the forum message board about the game.

The original post was a rambling question that seemed to be written by someone who was either too ecstatic about the game, or simply didn't know that it was best to refrain from run-on sentences, or both. She decided on both.

It read: *I got this game Comatose from the store it had a microphone with it, and it said it needed two people to play but it doesn't tell me what to do so can someone help me because I am lost?*

That wasn't the message board's troubling part, for if a child had picked the game up, he or she might not have gotten extremely far in it. What troubled her was that no one in the few responses seemed to know what the child was talking about. They had never heard of such a game before, and one even mocked the original poster for 'making it up.' Alexandra looked at the time stamp for the messages and sighed in defeat, for they were ten years old. She closed her laptop and decided to discuss it with her brother.

***

Ben heard rather than saw Alex walk back into the living room. He kept his gaze on the first chapter of his book. But he had stopped reading. Thoughts assaulted him instead. He guessed she wanted to talk about Tricia. Or maybe she wanted to talk about all the things he had refrained from talking about until now. He wasn't going to budge. He had nothing to say to her. No one deserved to hear his sorrows. No one had a right to them.

Maybe his twin sister did? No, that was just wishful thinking. She didn't need to be bogged down by his worries when she already had her own. She didn't show it, but he knew she had some. Why else would she have given up on pursuing dance when she had a chance to be an assistant teacher? She had chosen to work at that odd flower shop her friend had inherited instead.

Maybe he should ask her about it. That would be something worth conversing about. He knew enough about the shop to know Alex would have a new story or two to tell him about customers. He finally looked up from his book, just soon enough to see Alex enter the kitchen. So, she didn't want to talk. That made life considerably easier for him. He shook his head and got into a more comfortable position on the couch. He popped a Sweet Tart into his mouth and dispelled his thoughts with a mental shake of his head. Ben went back to reading.

***

Alexandra had walked into the living room and looked at her brother. He hadn't looked up from his book, but clearly he wasn't reading. She wanted to reach out to him, give him a hug, maybe let him cry; she knew he hadn't cried about it – since the one time he did, when it had happened and he couldn't contain himself – because he still had given her that same stony glare when she asked about it at the tea shop. Would she judge him, however, when the only people she had conversed about it with had been her therapist and a friend she hardly visited anymore?

No matter how long she had looked at him from her spot just inside the living room area, hand on the wall of the corridor, he hadn't looked up to meet her gaze. She could take it no longer and walked past him into the kitchen for a cup of tea. Barely thinking, hardly registering the smell of burnt lobster, automatically, she put the water to boil and found a mug. Then she remembered what she had planned on talking to him about: the odd forum board discussing the videogame *Comatose*, the game that had engrossed them both only moments before.

But it seemed he wasn't in a talking mood, so she made her tea in frustrated silence and walked past him once again, tugging against her instinct to sit by him on the big couch. She almost slammed her bedroom door behind her. Would she ever get through to him or would he ever allow it? She hadn't done anything to deserve his non-compliance, his silence, that death glare.

She had loved him as best she could, even though the only love she seemed to understand was someone else's rather than her own. That was why she had fit right in with the quaint store her friend owned, a bike-ride away from where she lived. She

had experienced pure glee when she took her extended holiday –
due to an accumulation of so many days off – to be there for her
brother while he searched for a job fresh out of college. But now
she was a bundle of confusion and almost tears, picking up her
smartphone for a distraction.

There were no new messages from the owner of the flower
shop, Brenda, which meant she wasn't needed in an emergency.
She had made it clear that she was available if such a need arose,
and now almost wished it had arisen. Could she bear her brother's
deathly silence about anything that mattered, anything but the
obscure videogame? Would he at least talk about the book he was
reading if she ever asked? Communication had been somewhat
complicated between them the last four years, with the only
topics of conversation being work or school. She was certain he
had at least two friends he had let go of who still lived where he
had gone to college, but she could barely remember their names,
which only showed how much he talked about them.

Now he was back in their hometown, crashing at her place.
She should feel happy that at least he was willing to do that: not
ignore her completely. She knew they needed each other, but she
couldn't tell how she would accomplish such a feat of help with
him acting the way he was. Where was carefree Ben? Talkative,
humorous Ben with his stupid jokes?

Alexandra could do nothing but sigh at the thought of the
ghost that was now her brother, someone who smiled as if by
accident, who argued quicker than he simply talked. She
understood love, but she had yet to understand how to get him
back in a state of happiness that would even border on the
possibility of loving and being loved. She did it with her
customers, but she couldn't do it with her own twin. Trying to get
rid of the feeling of utter failure (for it had been but a night and

day that he had been at her place), she checked her messages on her phone again – she had forgotten she was even holding her cellular device.

Alexandra realized she was still standing up in front of her medium-sized beanbag, and decided to sit down. There was a text message from a friend of hers, Andrea, asking to meet and catch up on life the day after tomorrow. Alexandra sat cross-legged on the beanbag, elbows poised on knees, back straight – like a proper dancer – and replied with an enthusiastic 'yes.' Which, of course, was more than just a simple 'yes,' for she was Alexandra, and nothing with Alexandra was ever simple. She allowed herself a weak smile while she browsed Tumblr, and looked forward to talking about anything at all with her brother the next day.

She hadn't realized when the sun had set, but she knew she had a few hours to go before sleep would take hold of her, so she kept busy with Tumblr, social media, a podcast or two, and a little bit of a book she had recently noticed was actually a romance novel. She was vexed by such a discovery, but called it research for work at Love & Flowers – where she helped customers with their relationships as well as selling them flowers – and read from it all the same.

Chapter 6

Ben yawned and scratched the stubble on his chin. The night before, he had hardly managed to fall asleep after many hours of insomnia. He couldn't even focus on rereading his favorite book, which never happened. So, he had taken another swig of wine and promised himself he would find sleep. Which he did after browsing Twitter, but it was fitful.

He didn't know what time it was and didn't care to know. Time was what he had the most of. His sister had made it clear he could stay as long as he liked. He was about to ask himself what he was doing with his life, when he remembered *Comatose*. That's what he was doing right now. Playing it and even letting himself enjoy it? He didn't know and didn't care to know. That had become a recurring thought with him.

He heard Alex singing a soft tune in the kitchen. "Alex?" he inquired. He was met with silence. "Alexandra?" he said a little louder. This time she answered. She appeared in the doorway.

"Yes, brother dear?" she said. She had a pot in her hand and was drying it as she spoke. The towel she used was bright orange. Of course it was. He mentally smiled, and almost didn't let it reach his lips. He turned his face from her to his fluffy pillow.

"How long have I been drooling?" he asked.

"Oh, I didn't mean to wake you. I've been trying to be as silent as a mouse."

"Mice aren't silent. And you were singing."

She grinned big. "Your ears are very keen," she said. She twirled back into the kitchen, her knee-length skirt billowing.

When she returned, her hands were free. "Last night's dishes are done."

"Breakfast?" he asked. "Had any?"

"I've been waiting for you. How does cereal sound, milord?" she asked, no sarcasm visible in her voice.

"Sounds like cereal."

She didn't reply and left him so she could rummage for it. He cocked his head and heard her close the fridge. She came back with the milk, two bowls, and two spoons. She placed them on the table. Alex looked at him, bewildered. "Oh! I forgot the cereal." She went back to get it. He chuckled, and it was barely audible. It would've been quite a feat to carry all three things at once, and he didn't put it past her. He regained his composure when she came back with the sugary meal.

"Move," she said. "Though it be a meager couch, it is *my* couch, sir, not yours."

Ben obliged and remembered. Yes, this was how she always talked. The eloquent speech of yesterday was not forced. He liked that about her. She knew she was a little odd, but didn't care. He reached for the red bowl. She quickly tapped his hand, in jest.

"You know that if something I put before us is red, it's mine. You're blue." She pointed at the blue bowl beside it. It was farther away from him.

"You were the one who put it in front of me," he said, hands shot up in mock indignation.

"You speak truth."

"Of course I do." He deliberately grabbed the blue bowl. It had some silver detailing to it.

He hadn't seen it before. Must be new. He looked at the cereal still clutched in her hand. "Gimme?"

Alexandra gave her brother the box of the too-sugary cereal, Lucky Charms. From her memories, it was as sugary as he liked it – at least the marshmallows were, which he always ate first – and she had bought it especially for him that very morning. They hardly had any of it at home growing up, since her parents had been all about health. This plan had back-fired on their only boy, who didn't suffer from weight-gain solely because he had a fast metabolism. He had sneaked sweets into the house whenever he could, eating it in secret and sharing it with his sisters.

"Do you recall when you bought your first box of Sweet Tarts?" she asked him, taking the box of cereal he had placed on the table beside his intricate tower. "You simply couldn't wrap your head around such tarty goodness, and I swear I thought you were going to switch from 'team sweet' to 'team tart.'"

"That was never gonna happen." He had already filled his bowl with cereal and milk and was spooning the sugary goodness into his mouth. The crunch made him smirk just a little. "Always loved these," he said.

She took the milk and poured into her own bowl. She hadn't failed to notice that he hadn't switched into anything that resembled pajamas before falling asleep the night before (he had slept in dark jeans), and hoped it was simply because he didn't own any. How was she to know? She had never thought of asking a customer, but she might. "Sir, do you own silk pajamas to fall asleep in, or are you more a same day clothes kind of guy?" she would say. She wasn't about to ask her brother that, either, though she very much wanted to. She let her mind wander.

"*Comatose!*" she blurted out before she knew what she was saying. "Yes, I looked it up last night—"

Her brother said mid-munch, making it a little hard to understand, "Don't tell me you've already looked up a walkthrough."

"You know me better than that," she said, finally putting her spoon in her meal. She crossed her legs, balanced her bowl on her skirt, and told him all about what she had discovered the night before. There wasn't much to report, but she did it all the same, with a slight frown on her face. She acknowledged to herself that maybe this wasn't as interesting a line of conversation as she thought, and reached the end of what she had to say. Alexandra finally focused her eyes on her brother.

"Whoa," he said, quickly putting his bowl on the table beside his wallet, almost knocking over his Sweet Tarts. He picked one up absently and popped it into his mouth, sucking on it. "That was the only thing you found on the game?" he asked, clearly awestruck. "That's ridiculous. You must've missed something."

"Nope," she said resolutely before putting a spoon of Lucky Charms into her mouth. She glanced at him, at her bowl, back at him, chewing. "I tried everything, even Tumblr," she said as she finished her mouthful.

"That's ridiculous," he reiterated.

"I did hear you the first time," she said, with a grin she couldn't contain. He was hooked and she knew he knew it.

"I was going to ask you about Love & Flowers, but this is far more interesting."

She sat aghast. How dare he? "How dare you?" she said. "Love & Flowers is always interesting." He had wanted to talk about her job, which was what held her more aghast than her statement, but she didn't let that show.

"I know, I know," he said, worrying with his spoon. "But *Comatose* being basically a phantom game? That's, well, absurd. Do you think there's only one or two of them out there? But if there were, surely Wikipedia would have something on it."

"Nothing of the kind," Alexandra said, "Wikipedia, I mean." She burrowed holes into her cereal with her gaze, thinking about his question. The thought had crossed her mind, but it had been a thought too ludicrous to entertain for more than a quick second. "I'm thinking you're right; it must be the only copy. Or one of the only copies, something fantastical as that. I had my doubts…"

"What have you done?" Ben asked. "Have you answered the forum?"

"I found it rather pointless, considering the question was made ten years ago." She picked up a red Sweet Tart and plopped it into the cereal because why not? Stranger things had already happened, and last night's queries were proof of it. Besides, she'd always wondered if Sweet Tarts would bleed out in milk like Skittles – probably not, but it never hurt to try, as any idle time was worth making into an experiment.

"Now we've *got* to finish it," Ben told her. She saw that he was grinning, and counted it another small triumph. She also noticed him getting up. "Laptop in room, yes?" he asked, standing and walking toward her room.

She grabbed his shirtsleeve before he could move any further. "Nope, nope, nope, sir. You must first freshen up. No one is walking into my room with bad breath. Besides, there's still too much cereal in your bowl for you to cease breakfasting. Patience is a virtue."

He sighed and sat back down. "Yes, mother," he grumbled.

"Thank you," she said with a decided smirk. She pointed at his bowl. "Eat up."

***

Ben had to go through the motions of eating, a shower, and teeth-brushing before his sister allowed him to even see her laptop again. He left his toothbrush in the bathroom this time, rather than the living room table. He was starting to feel at home. She fetched her laptop from her room and plugged it to the TV with the HDMI cable. Alex split the screens like before and handed him the laptop, keeping the microphone and mouse to herself.

"Walk around Solstice," she told Jack. He obeyed.

Ben wandered his three available hallways – the first longer one, and the two that branched out of its left side.

Alex sighed. "Where should we go next?" she asked.

Ben looked closely to the three dark red-spined books, one of them still completely blank. He looked at the TV screen. "What was that big building?" He had seen it down one of the many streets in Jack's trip around the town.

"I can't be certain until I go to it," she replied.

He popped a Sweet Tart into his mouth. The tower was slowly dwindling. That was okay because he knew where to buy more. He should ask Alex if they had any need to buy groceries, but that could be done later.

"Go to the big building?" Alex said into the microphone. They were still unclear which commands Jack would or wouldn't obey. He obeyed this one and walked, gait almost uncertain, until the big building. He stood in front of it. "Walk in," she said. He took a step forward but hesitated. He stopped.

Curious, Ben walked with the arrow keys down the lit hallways on his screen. He couldn't be sure, but he thought he saw a new one all alight. He found it next to the playground hallway. He walked in. As he did so, he glimpsed Jack move. Just in time to see him stop on the front steps. Jack looked down at his feet. They were in dusty tennis shoes. Light erupted from where he stood, painting the drab yellow of dust into the sleek grey of cement. The color went up the steps, to the building. Glass double doors appeared where a hole had gaped in the front of the building.

They heard Jack speak. *"'Got a class?' I interjected and awkwardly straightened my backpack straps on my shoulders."*

Then the screen blinked three times, and each time it was brighter. Jack was in water once again, struggling to breath.

"Damn it," Ben said in indignation. His screen went black, and then he was back at the starting point of his hallways.

"Swim to shore!" Alex said beside him. "Please do ascertain what we still have before cursing in my humble abode," she said to Ben.

Ben opened the *Kat* book. The scene they had gotten of the playground was still there, which was an encouraging sign. He walked down a hallway and noticed that the *Playground* book now had a *1* after its title. He should've noticed if this was true earlier as well. Ben chastised himself inwardly. No matter. With a little difficulty, he navigated the corridors until he found the last one that had appeared. He looked at the one dark red book on the shelves, in the midst of the drab rainbow of the rest of the books. He glanced at the TV screen.

Jack was already back on land, facing *Tom's Café*. Ben must've been too focused on his side of the game to have heard her order him over.

"Oh," he said. "You're ahead of me. I was going to say that I found the book for this one. I'm going to call it *School*." He typed it in, but the letters blurred, and *College* showed up in place of what he had written. No matter. "How come we didn't unlock a new memory?" he asked as an afterthought.

"We must assume we missed something," said Alex, "or he wouldn't have blacked out again. I thought it best if I looked for a backpack, like we found that Styrofoam cup."

"Good thinking," said Ben. Jack must've overheard yet again, because he had walked into the coffee-shop, this time through what was the front door. He had started searching. "Please tell me I'm not the only one still creeped out by that."

"You are not," she replied.

Ben strained his neck forward, eager, and followed Jack's search. The character looked at each object he passed and stepped over, a second each. He must've looked through the entire store: Ben saw objects he hadn't seen before. A new piece of art on the counter, a teddy bear under a chair, cheerleader pom-poms hung on a hook, part of a wire fence close to the hole in the wall, a bottle of half-empty orange juice, a piece of wood in a corner. But no backpack. "What's up with that?" he asked his sister. Ben was seated on the floor in front of the couch again. He glanced up and over at her. She had an expression of worry on her face.

"I can't be certain," she said, "but I think he didn't find what we were looking for."

"Maybe he didn't hear you right."

"By all means," she said, and handed him the microphone. He straightened himself, legs under the table, back on the wine-colored couch's bottom half.

"Look for a backpack," Ben said into the mic with a clear voice.

Jack started searching again and stopped suddenly. "I have," he said through the laptop speakers.

"Are you sure?" Ben asked with a wince in his voice.

Jack didn't answer. He stood there, looking at the wall where a piece of abstract art hung crooked. *Dumb question,* Ben thought.

"Okay," Ben said to no one in particular. "Now what?"

***

The voices tell me to walk around Solstice again. They are clearly more lost than I am, but I'm a puppet on a string. I'm dead inside, and each new thought found is a victory. But it hurts so much. How can anything hurt so much?

"Go to the big building?" the female voice asks clearly, quizzically. The voice is kind and uncertain. I almost chuckle at such naiveté. I find the art building with ease, for I am, in a way I can't really express, happy to be going there.

"Walk in," commands the voice. But something is still not right. I take a step forward and stop. This shouldn't be happening yet. But the voice beckoned, so I must go all the same. I walk until I'm on the front steps. And I remember. The bright colors strike me for a second or two.

"Got a class?" I interjected, and awkwardly straightened my backpack straps on my shoulders.

No. This isn't right. I'm not ready for this yet.

The sun is blinding, and I'm treading water again.

I can't remember what my last thought was, but the voice tells me to swim back to the fire-bathed speck of a town. Then I remember her in the playground and a thought of studying.

Still musing over this, I head over to Tom's Café. My haven. The voices that guide me talk about finding a backpack, and so I walk in and begin my search. I know where it is, but I refuse to look for it. The timing is all wrong. So, instead, I pretend to look.

The voices are as confused as I am certain that they are leading me the wrong way. So, when the male voice asks me to look for the backpack again, I almost obey. But I stop. I've looked for it as much as I will look for it at present. From this I have

86

gathered that they can't make me do everything. Good.

"Are you sure?" *the male voice pipes up again.*

I stare at the wall that holds a familiar painting near a familiar chair in an all-too-familiar café and don't answer. I am not obligated to. This is my world, not theirs. Let's keep it that way.

"Now what?" *he asks.*

***

Alexandra was at a loss as to what they must do and noticed this was becoming a trend with *Comatose.* She would have to thank the makers of such a splendorous game if she ever found out who they were, for a game that made you think at every turn was a game worth playing.

She had the mouse on the notebook again on her lap, and her feet were touching the floor. She swayed her torso from one side to the other once, trying to make way for new thoughts and possible solutions. She made Jack look around him with the mouse and he stopped when he was looking over his shoulder, then, without her needing to direct him, he looked forward again at the wall that had the painting on it. She could tell the painting was an abstract splash of colors, but Jack couldn't seem to focus his gaze on it; his vision only blurred when he looked at the painting. She conceded that this was rather odd, but, in short, this was an odd game.

Alexandra looked at Ben and the progress he might quite possibly be making as she sat and did much of nothing. He had found a new book with *College* on its red spine, and before she could say anything contrary to what he was about to do, he opened the virtual book and typed in *Class, backpack.* The words parted and made way for the rest of the snippet of a scene: *'Got a class?' I interjected, and awkwardly straightened my backpack straps on my shoulders.*

"Jackpot!" said Ben, and it became clear to her that this was the only way they were allowed to celebrate anything in this game. She grinned at her brother, and he glanced at her. "What?" he asked. "I got it right."

"We don't have the full scene yet, and I doubt we would have it even if we went back to the college building. It didn't seem right, the fact that the TV screen blinked thrice, and I am wondering what we're still missing."

"It's got to be the backpack," her brother said, hands thrown up in exasperation, a glint of fury in his mismatched eyes.

She put a finger to her closed lips, thinking furiously. They had looked for it in this game's 'lost and found,' AKA *Tom's Café*. They were still in it, and yet Jack hadn't found it. Maybe there was another place like this one in the game, another place to look for scene-unlocking objects? Where could that place be? It couldn't be a house, or could it? It couldn't be the first house, for they couldn't get near it without Jack going straight back into sea. She thought she saw another, smaller building with a sign that would've been neon if the entire place hadn't been taken over by dust. It might be worth checking out.

"Ben," Alexandra finally said, out of her reverie, "how about we try out a new building? There was a small one with a neon sign in the door that I think might be another place where we can look for said backpack. Walk out of the café." She had taken the microphone from where Ben had placed it beside him on the floor, and had said the last sentence into it for Jack to hear loud and clear. "Go to the neon sign building," she continued resolutely.

It could be her impression, but it seemed like Jack quickened his pace to get to it. As soon as he had it in his sights, she told him to walk into it. When he walked over the dusty front steps, he stopped for a second, and she thought he would black out again. So, she said, "Keep going!" into his 'ear,' and he obeyed, though somewhat reluctantly.

Jack walked into what was clearly a bar. There were no windows, so the only natural light there came in from the wide-open, glass front door, which was missing a piece on the left-hand corner. There were three gold-dust-covered tables in the enclosed space, and bar stools faced a counter that somehow looked stickier than it did dusty. Behind the counter were an assortment of bottles for drink making, each with its lid off. The open door illuminated a rectangle of concentrated Solstice sunlight over what looked like an empty space at the counter, where a barstool should be.

Jack had been looking around the place on his own as soon as he entered, and his gaze fixed on the empty spot. "Where is she?" he asked in a low tone. Then again, "Where is she?" louder this time. "I need to find her."

"Who?" Alexandra asked him earnestly. "Is it Kat you're looking for?"

Jack nodded once as a reply, and she would've missed it if she weren't intently looking at the TV screen.

"New hallway!" Ben announced from his place on the floor. Alexandra leaned closer in to the table, where her brother had put her sleek laptop. "There's a red book here," he hovered to it, already naming it *Bar*. "But we have no snippet yet. Walk to the empty space, maybe?"

"What if it makes him uneasy and blink out again? He doesn't seem too put-together at the moment."

Ben put one hand up, as if to say, 'no harm in trying.'

***

Ben looked at his red spine and then back to the TV screen.

"Go to the empty space by the counter," Alex told Jack. He obliged, perhaps a little too quickly.

Jack walked until he was almost at the empty space. Before he could reach it, a black barstool materialized there. He stopped and blinked. When he opened his eyes, dim, yellow light had erupted from the lamps above. The counter looked cleaner now. The ghost of a girl was perched precariously on the barstool. Her hair was a mess of unkempt curls, and she wore a red dress.

She reeked of vodka and looked like she would fall off her barstool if she weren't holding on with one hand, Jack said. He blinked again. The bar went back to what it was. The barstool was missing again, along with the girl. But to Ben's surprise, Jack didn't 'reset' the game. He seemed to be okay, though he shook a little before he stood still again. The yellow light had disappeared, and the girl too. The bar had gone back to dusty.

"So," Ben said, "are we going in the right direction? He seems A-Okay." Ben glanced up to Alex. She was standing. Her hand held the microphone limply, and she had placed the mouse on the table. She was silent for a few moments.

"In the last memory," she finally said, "they seemed awfully young to be at a bar, so this can't be right. But how come he didn't black out?"

"Maybe this is the next memory in the sequence."

"Perhaps." Alex sat down again, her legs crossed. Ben thought she looked disappointed. For some reason. "Maybe that is why he almost achieved the memory at the entrance? I simply didn't let him go through with it."

"You know how we'll find out?" Ben asked her. He crossed his legs as well, still seated on the floor.

"By putting a memory into your *Bar* book?"

He wrote 'vodka,' 'barstool,' and 'hand' into the *Bar* book. As soon as he did so, the words separated. The rest of the sentence filled in for him: *She reeked of vodka and looked like she would fall off her barstool if she weren't holding on with one hand.*

"Everything under control?" he asked Alex. They both stared at the screen, but nothing else happened.

"I do think it is!" she replied with glee. He looked at her. She had a smile on. He snickered softly. "Safe and sound!" his sister exclaimed. "We have a barstool to find."

***

Alexandra was ecstatic that they seemed to be getting the hang of the game. Or maybe they were finally getting lucky. Either way, she was happy for the both of them, as Ben seemed to be cheering up considerably due to their achievements. She sat back down on the sofa, contented, and grabbed Ben's fluffy white pillow, hugging it to her chest.

"We have a barstool to find?" she brought up again, looking into his mysterious eyes.

"Yup," he replied. "The mic is all yours." He rose and sat on the wine-colored couch beside her, arms propped up on the upper side of the couch's top cushion, hands slack beside him.

She picked the microphone up from where she had abandoned it on the low table. She put the pillow on her skirted lap, picked up the laptop, and brought it to her with the microphone well attached. The pillow served as a buffer between the laptop's growing heat and her skirt. Alexandra looked at the computer's battery bar, which was closer to low than high.

"I do believe we are in dire need of the laptop's charger if we plan on continuing," she said to Ben before flitting into her room to get the charger. She found it through the little light that came through her curtains, and the whole while she thought, *Benjamin is happy while he plays, so let's keep him playing.* She barely registered everything else in her room, including her neatly made bed, and was already back in the living room, plugging the charger into the wall and into her laptop.

"There you go," she said, and sat down with the pillow, laptop, and microphone on her lap yet again.

"That was quick," Ben remarked. He had not changed positions, and she wondered when his arms would tire from that awful position, but she didn't mention it.

"I pride myself on being efficient," Alexandra replied with a small smile, but she received none in return. Perhaps she was wrong about her brother's happiness.

"Barstool?" he asked.

"Barstool," she acquiesced. "Go back to *Tom's Café* and walk in," she said into the microphone. She watched as Jack left the bar and found his way back to the café without a hesitant step, which confirmed to her that they were indeed headed in the right direction. He walked in and stood still, looking at the array of objects in front of him. Alexandra quickly spotted it: a barstool covered with dust at one of the tables, looking out of place with the wooden café chairs around it. Unlike the chairs, the stool had nothing piled on top of it, and she found it to be dark green rather than black under all that dust. This was odd, but it only made her more certain that it was what they had to do next, and she told

Jack to walk toward the barstool, which he did in two long strides, walking over a big cushion.

Like with the Styrofoam cup before it, Jack reached out and touched the barstool, and an image took over the screen. He was at the yellow-lit bar, but this time he was looking at the floor, to a gleaming zipper that belonged to what looked like a small purse. Words appeared on the upper part of the TV screen, and Jack read them aloud: *I saw its zipper glisten on the grimy floor.*

The image faded away and the dusty, object-laden café was back onscreen. Jack had a hand wrapped around the barstool, now black and clean, and hugged it toward his chest.

"Did he sound more adult to you?" Alexandra asked Ben, glancing at him. He had moved his arms to lay down on either side of him, and she smiled inwardly at her prophecy fulfilled.

"I think so, yeah," he answered.

"To the bar!" she said into the microphone. Jack not only walked to it, but he walked right in instead of hesitating at the entrance like he had before. This man was clearly on a mission, and he strode until he was a step away from the empty space by the counter. "Place the barstool down," Alexandra told him, and he put it down carefully, then looked up at one of the lamps that hung from the ceiling as it burst into dim yellow light. Jack blinked and he was looking at a drunk Kat perched on the barstool. Alexandra, eagerly, looked at the laptop screen on her lap, and saw that Ben was doing the same. The *Bar 2* book slid out of its place on the bookshelf and opened to a page toward the middle. She didn't recall her brother putting in the *2* next to *Bar,* but her thought was arrested by what was happening on the page. Conversation and narration were suddenly there, and the twins looked up in time to see it play out on the TV screen as an older-sounding Jack read the scene aloud:

***

"*Heya... Zack,*" *Kat slurred out.* "*No, that didn't sound right. Z... J... Jack. There you go. Heya, you got my message.*"

"*You called me,*" *I said.* "*Which I'm glad for.*"

"*Oh.*" *She was clearly beyond drunk. She reeked of vodka and looked like she would fall off her barstool if she weren't holding on with one hand. I couldn't see her too well in the dimly-lit bar, but I could tell she was doing worse than ever. Her long, dark-red, spaghetti-strap dress looked stained of drink, her hair was a mess of unkempt curls, and her cheeks were red.* "*Want a drink?*" *she asked.*

"*No,*" *I replied. She looked at me and I could see that her green eyeshadow was smeared.*

"*Shame,*" *she said.* "*We were having so much fun! Right, Jimmy?*" *she asked the bartender. She was one of the only people left at the bar. It was nearing two a.m.*

"*I gave her water, man,*" *Jimmy said apologetically, pointing at the full glass in front of her.* "*She wouldn't take it.*" *That usually meant he had stopped giving her drinks. I silently thanked him for it.*

"*That's okay, Jim, thanks,*" *I said. It was too late for this nonsense. I was in my pajamas. I looked over at Kat. She had slumped in her chair and seemed to be dozing. But her arm held her still, even in her stupor. I poked her in the shoulder.* "*Hey,*" *I murmured,* "*did you at least pay?*" *She jerked awake.* "*I did, I did,*" *Kat protested. Jimmy shook his head and slid me over a receipt. Her tab was in no ways short, but she was in no condition to pay. So I did it for her. She had closed her eyes.*

"*Hey,*" *I shook her. Her dark eyes snapped open.* "*I'm*

94

taking you home."

"Good," she said, and tried to get up. She lost her balance and leaned on my shoulder. "He's so sweet," she told Jimmy. "So sweet. And sexy." She put her other hand on my chest. "Eyes off," she said.

I pried her hand loose. "Come on," I said. "You're making a fool of yourself," I told her in a low voice.

"Jimmy don't give a fuck right, Jimmy?" she said. "No fuck Jimmy!" At this, she promptly threw up. She rubbed her mouth with a hand. "Whoops," she said.

"Oh gosh," I said. "I am so sorry, Jim." I looked over at him.

Jimmy shook his head and went into a back room. "I'm used to cleaning up barf," he said, his voice a little distant. He emerged with a mop and bucket. "Besides, we have worse," he assured me. He walked around the counter and started cleaning up. I felt an urge to help him, but there was no time to waste. I needed to take Kat home.

"Where's your purse?" I asked her, voice raised so I could make sure she heard.

"I 'ono," she said.

"Think she threw it on the ground after calling you," Jimmy said, pointing. I saw its zipper glisten on the grimy floor. I made Kat sit back down and bent to pick it up.

"So sexy," she said, looking at me crouched over. I grimaced at Jimmy as an apology and a thank you. He held up his hand in recognition. I put my arm around Kat's waist to keep her steady and got her to stand. "Sexy Jack come home with me," she whispered.

"This isn't flirting," I told her. "This is me making sure you're safe."

"Uhum," she said under her breath. She was falling asleep standing up. We walked out of the bar into the lit street, and she winced at the streetlamps. *"Turn 'em off,"* she said.

"No," I responded. I half-carried her to my car. I placed her in the passenger seat and nudged a leg with a finger. *"Legs in."* She obeyed. But she gripped my wrist.

"Cuddle my house?" she asked. She sounded like a little girl asking a friend over for tea.

"You know we don't cuddle."

"Mah," she scoffed. *"So touchy."*

I pulled my wrist out of her hold. *"Seat belt on,"* I said, and closed the passenger door. I went into the driver's seat. She looked so vulnerable, almost asleep, helpless. No sense in asking her why she felt like she needed to overdrink alone. She generally knew her limits. She tended to call me to drink, not after.

She hadn't buckled herself in, so I clicked the seatbelt gingerly into place for her. Kat leaned back and got comfortable, a cat in a ray of sunshine. I drove halfway to her place before she spoke in her sleep.

"Max," she mumbled. *"No. Max!"* she cried. I'd never heard that name before.

Something must've happened to him. Maybe that's why she'd left all those years ago.

I got to her place and pushed at the door. It was unlocked and swung open. I pulled her into her house, her feet dragging, ruining her sandals. I plopped her down on the living room couch, found a small throw pillow and placed it under her head. I put my jacket on her. She snuggled up quickly. I found her key in her purse, walked out, locked the door, and slipped the key under the door. But I couldn't leave her alone – not in this state. So, I made myself comfortable in my car, ears sensitive to any *sound, and slept fitfully until daybreak. Then I drove away.*

***

"Jackpot?" Alexandra asked as she glanced at her twin brother.

"Jackpot," Ben agreed, looking back at her.

No need for her to ask Ben anymore; some men did own pajamas. But she had one new question: "Who's Max?"

"Darned if I know," Ben replied.

***

I know what the neon sign means, for it involves her need for me. But this bar looks broken, like everything else on this desolate planet. We were so young back then… And if I follow through the patch of light… She must've hidden herself from this sun-soaked place by going into this darkened, lonely place. But why am I not with her? What has happened? In a flash, I remember:

"She reeked of vodka and looked like she would fall off her barstool if she weren't holding on with one hand." You were meant to call me before you reached this point of no return. But more pressing matters are at hand, for in a second she is gone, replaced by dust and sunlight.

Why am I being pulled toward the café? There is no way I will find her there – she had a dislike for the place. Perhaps my luck will turn. I thought I had glimpsed something…

Yes, the barstool! Where is her purse? I just saw her purse! Where is she? Please lead me to her, for there is no time to waste. Though I cannot see it, the neon sign of the bar beckons. I hurry toward it, through its hinged glass to the empty spot overtaken by daylight. I put your barstool in place and finally see you, your thin nose, upturned, and you're speaking to me.

I manage to take you home, to safety. I am ready to return to that hell-hole.

***

Ben was astounded to say the least. They had found a new memory. He hadn't even needed to put in the second memory snippet. He wondered why and was about to ask his sister about it. She looked as flabbergasted as he was. He decided not to ask.

"So," he said, to break the silence. "Who is this Kat person?"

"A young girl with curly hair, a need for drink, and she recently acquired a taste for green eyeshadow." Alex enumerated on her fingers.

"I know all that," Ben said, fighting a smile. "Who is she to Jack?"

"She is certainly not his girlfriend; that much I know to be true," she said. Alex looked into his eyes, and it was disconcerting. He looked away, to the laptop still on her lap.

"Did something new happen on my end?" he asked Alex.

As a reply, she handed him the laptop. The mic stayed with her.

The *Bar 2* book in his hands was heavy with the scene they had uncovered. He hadn't written the *2* in, but since Alex hadn't mentioned it, neither would he. He put it back in its place on the bookshelf. "How do I access Kat's book?" he asked sheepishly.

"Perhaps if you press ENTER, you will find it."

He did so and found both the book and the fountain pen slotted away in the corner. He opened the *Kat* book, but the bar memory had not emerged in it. He closed it, even more confused. He pressed ENTER and stared at the red spine of the *Bar 2* book.

"It didn't transfer," he said, thoughtful. "How come?"

"As they say, 'your guess is as good as mine.' But—" And here she stopped talking. He could see the cogs in her head turning, and looked at the TV screen. He placed the laptop on the low table – it pulled the mic with it. He caught it before it fell and placed it on the laptop's keyboard. Standing up, he walked around the table and stood before the television screen. Jack had moved.

He was now at the curtained house they had gone to earlier, where the memory had left him. And he was blinking. With haste, Ben turned, picked up the microphone and said, "Go to the playground!" It had been the first place he had thought of. Thankfully, Jack walked long steps away from the damning house. He found the playground and stood outside of it. It might've been his impression, but it seemed that Jack was breathing short breaths. They calmed into steady ones as he looked toward the ground.

"What was that?" Alex asked him. Clearly, she had been so caught up in her thoughts that she had missed the reset that was about to happen.

"I just saved our skins," Ben said, looking at her. "He was at Kat's again."

"Oh. Sorry, Jack," she said, looking at the computer screen. "I was thinking, Ben, that we need to put these memories in order. It is wrong to think that Kat would go from contraband beer to being in a bar, getting quite drunk."

"You're right," Ben said. Why hadn't he thought of that himself? "So. What do we have to work with?"

"The college snippets, dunce cap."

"Other than those."

"A big cemetery of discarded items in something that used

to be a quaint café belonging to a man named Tom."

"And a mystery."

"I don't follow."

"What the deuce is the relationship between Kat and Jack? I get the feeling they want to be more than friends, but they're not. So, what happened to stop them?"

"Good question," Alex said. She looked quizzically at Ben and the TV screen from her place on the couch. "What is it indeed?"

Ben sighed. "Go find the college book for me, will ya?" he asked of her, sounding defeated. At least he felt it. He wasn't sure what he felt was conveyed by his words, wishing it wasn't. Alex either didn't notice or didn't care for his tone of voice. She guided the entity and waited. The laptop was still on the table, and she had to reach over from her place on the couch to get there.

Ben went back to his seat on the sofa. He took the computer from the table. He opened the red cover of *College* and read what was written in it. "We need to find that backpack," he said.

"Yes sir!" Alex said with some glee. They were on a roll, and she knew it. He was more skeptical. But he waited anyway.

Alex sent Jack through the front door of the coffee shop. She was clever this time. "Overturn objects to find the backpack," she said into the mic. To Ben's surprise, Jack obeyed. He looked under chairs, in corners, until he finally found a well-worn Jansport. It came as no surprise to him that Jack would have a simple backpack as this one. He seemed like a fairly no-nonsense man.

Jack picked the backpack up from under a huge stuffed bear, and placed its straps on his shoulders. Dust unsettled from it and seemed to fill Jack's entire vision with gold. It was as if all the dust from the café decided to spring up at once. Jack blinked it away and rubbed his eyes.

When he looked up again, he was at the college steps, facing what seemed to be a sober Kat. Words sprung up: *But that single dimple on her right cheek appeared when she noticed who it was, her mouth open in surprise.* Then he blinked hard, and the scene changed, dust settling back onto the crowded café.

"Dimple, noticed, surprised," Ben said to himself as soon as the fountain pen appeared in his character' sights. He typed the words in, and the sentence fit itself snugly in between.

"Onward, to college!" Alex exclaimed, fist in the air. She smiled big, happy.

"Onward, onward," Ben repeated with little enthusiasm.

"What's the matter, brother dear?"

"It doesn't seem like the next memory," said Ben, "something is missing. I can feel it." He took a Sweet Tart into his mouth and sucked on it. Now it was time for *him* to be thoughtful, and she let him.

When he looked up, Jack was nearing the front steps of the college building. He didn't waver, but stood on the front steps. He looked outward, at Solstice, and turned his gaze to the ground in front of him. He seemed to be thinking. Then the scene played out and the dust that had goldened the ground was gone.

***

It was the first time I'd seen her since she left town six years ago without a goodbye.

When she hadn't arrived to our usual hangout that Wednesday night, I had gone to her school the next day and asked around. All they had said was that her mom had called about transferring her to a different state. I didn't even have her cell phone number.

I didn't expect to meet her again, especially not at our town's small college. I recognized her instantly by her curly, deep, chestnut-colored hair. She still walked a leisurely yet confident stride, like she had no place to be but was determined to get there.

She had grown out of the mane she used to sport when we were teenagers. Her hair was longer and flowed like a rippling river. She wore dark, green flats and her black, sleeveless blouse was tucked into her smart-fitting jeans. I saw her hesitate as she took to the steps of the arts building. Something was not right with Kat.

"Hey!" I said. "Where've you been?"

She turned to look at me. Her entire face displayed confusion. But that single dimple on her right cheek appeared when she noticed who it was, her mouth open in surprise. "Jack?" she said. I could smell the slightest whiff of alcohol on her breath, and its sweet smell made me want to ask so many questions. Too much must've happened since our coffee-fueled nights. She sat down on the steps. "God, I thought I would never find old friends."

I took that as an invitation and sat beside her, but not too close. "I didn't know you went here," I said. "I'm surprised I haven't seen you." People were starting to dodge around us to get into the building for their classes, but I didn't mind. I had found Kat again and I wasn't going to let the connection vanish. I wasn't going to let six years of silence sour her return.

"I just transferred, dummy," she said. The name-calling was new. She put a stray curl behind her ear.

"In your... last semester of senior year?" I asked. The crowd was dimming now. I was late for my Art Appreciation class, but I had perfect attendance so far, so it didn't matter.

"There's no law against it," she scoffed.

"Well..." I pondered. "It isn't normal."

"You know I don't do normal," she said and threw her head back. That usually meant she was done talking. She got up.

"Got a class?" I interjected and awkwardly straightened my backpack straps on my shoulders.

"No, dummy," she said. She had found a new nickname for me. "I'm an art student. We live in this building."

"Oh," I said. Obviously. "I do philosophy."

She smirked. "Of course, you do."

I followed her into the large building. She was headed up the art studio steps.

"You got a class?" she huffed, annoyed. I was hoping she would be happier to see me, but was unclear as to why she was back in the first place. She always looked a little sad, even when happy. This was different, a sort of unforgiving bitterness.

"I do," I said. "But it's Mueller. He can wait," I added, trying to keep the mood light. She didn't respond but kept on going up, like I wasn't there.

"Can I come see your space?" I ventured.

"I've only got one project finished." She looked at me with a glare in her deep eyes, like she was trying to decide if I was worth keeping around. I made puppy eyes. Something I'm not proud of, but it worked. "Fine," she conceded. "But only for a minute." She climbed the last step into the art studio hall. "I work alone."

***

Benjamin had been right after all, for six years had passed since Jack had seen his friend last, although they seemed to have more of a history than a meeting at a playground when teens. They still had to find the rest of the meetings, the Wednesday ones that Jack had mentioned. This made her glad, for this made it a puzzle game, like she had thought. They were finding the memories in all the wrong orders, and yet these same memories were appearing before them, as if asking to be placed correctly. As if Jack were asking them for help. She sat still, looking at the TV screen, waiting for something – anything – to explain Kat to her. She wanted to know her secrets, the same as Jack. The same way she wanted to know what was going on in her twin brother's head. Neither would talk, and she let out a deep breath.

"She reminds me of you, Ben," Alexandra said, not sure of how loudly she wanted to be saying it, unsure of how he would react.

"Really?" Ben interjected. "I hadn't noticed." His voice held some sincerity, some scorn, and a little glimmer of hope, though faint. "So, they met again in college," he was already saying. "But they are still friends, right?" Alexandra expected him to finish the sentence with 'or is that Jack's wishful thinking?'

He let the question hang in the air, like a small elephant wrapped in a neat bow. "If you are suggesting he has been friend-zoned, I might have to agree with you," Alexandra said carefully, treading around the corners of the elephant. She threw him a line of bait, saying, "I've rejected guys before, if you care to know. It wasn't easy doing, but it was a necessity."

"Do expound, your majesty," he said with some mockery in his voice, but he mostly seemed genuine, and so she went with that.

"Oh, dear," she said. "I wasn't sure you were actually going to be interested. I need to disentangle it in my head first. One moment." Alexandra picked up the pillow and hugged it to her chest, caught very much off guard, and she did not like the feeling. She let her brain wander to the right memory, of a man at her workplace.

"Well," she started, as all good storytellers do. "I was working at Love & Flowers, and he was one of my first steady clients. He always seemed to come in for help about a different girl. Once she was named Stacey, the other Mary, the other Kelly, and so on."

"So, he was a womanizer," Ben took her silence and filled it. He put his hands on his knees, cross-legged. "I hope you kicked his ass out of there. Your store isn't for people like him."

Alexandra was grateful that he had concluded, on his own, that her store was meant for men in serious relationships, possibly marriage, who needed some female guidance about how to act toward such an engagement. "Alas, dear brother, this wasn't his type. He had simply wandered into the store looking for someone to love. I only noticed when it was too late, and he had understood my 'help' as casual flirting."

"Uh-oh," Ben said on cue. He sat with his back to the couch arm that had been beside him and leaned forward to listen more closely.

"I don't know if all the different girls did exist," Alexandra continued, "but I am quite sure they didn't. His sob stories were always very vague, as if he was making them up on the spot. He never bought anything and didn't even seem interested in our many chocolates, cards, and flowers. I only took note of his interest when he bought a red rose for me after I had suggested it. It had a note on it that said "'Til next time?'"

"Nope, jump right out of that," Ben said, shaking his head.

"I did, as quickly as possible, like a cat out of water," she concluded.

"You may think yourself a cat, Alexandra, but you do not have their reflexes."

"I know," she said, and playfully punched him in the arm. "I learned to watch out after that, for my guard had been very much down since I started the job. I was, to put it bluntly, very naïve. But your sister has learned her lesson, not to fret." She put the pillow back on her lap, smoothed its pillow case, cold to her fingers.

"Good," he said, and he did sound relieved. She silently thanked him for it, for since they were children, he was the first to understand her and leave her well alone when she made mistakes such as these. She had missed his friendship all those years he was away in college, barely visiting, and she was only taking note of it now, like she had awoken from a dream that didn't include him and realized now that this – them sitting on this couch and playing a computer game together – was reality. She was going to cling to it as best she could, for her time off was long, but not infinite. Then and there, she promised herself she would get to the bottom of this – the game, Ben's bitterness toward life – before he left, for she knew not where.

She must've been silent for too long, for he was looking at her with those heterochromatic eyes, searching her face for something. Anything he could react to. She smiled and pointed an accusing finger at him. "Your turn," she said, for it was only fair. Her brother didn't think as she did, for he shook his head, as if in protest. She lowered her finger and stared into his eyes for a second too long. "Oh, Ben, I'm curious now. Don't leave me hanging."

"Why am I on the stand here?"

"Because we never talk about this type of thing. I told you about when I rejected a guy. And you tell me about getting rejected."

"Mine hurt more than yours," he said, getting up from the sofa to walk about the room. He did this when he was feeling uncomfortable, when he didn't want to talk. In her mind, she urged him to fight against it, and she could see him glancing toward her every now and again as he paced. She kept her gaze on his trek, not breaking eye contact with his face.

"Okay," he said finally, but he didn't go back to his seat beside her on the sofa. Distance, then, would be the circumstance of this revelation. She had to content herself with it, and so she did. He stopped, back to the TV, the little table that still held dirty cereal bowls between them. She must remember to put them away, but it would have to wait.

"This one girl, I, well, I dated her."

Alexandra already had a myriad of questions. But she pursed her lips and said nothing, which was very hard for her to do.

"Uhm… second year? Of college. We, well, we dated for a year and look I'm sorry I didn't tell you but I just—"

She put a hand up to stop him. "No judgment, no pity, Alexandra style."

"Okay. Okay, well, we dated for a year. I'm not sure… exactly why she wanted to date me. She was one of the only female chemical engineering majors who attended the same classes as I did. There were better men than me to date. But, well, I don't know. It's a mystery."

"Yes, you can move on," Alexandra said with a smile, and she was surprised that she meant it. She knew what to do and now she just needed to let it flow.

"She was the one of the prettiest girls I've ever seen. Which I don't say about many girls. As I'm sure you know. If you remember."

"I do, yes. You don't easily form crushes, not even when you were a budding teenager."

"Yeah. And I thought she was the one. I truly did." Here, he crossed his arms over his chest, and she didn't like it, for it meant he was shielding himself. But, like any other customer of hers, she let him, as long as he kept talking.

"She was smart, laughed at my jokes, understood my taste in movies, my chemistry hobbies, and we really seemed to connect. But I guess we didn't, 'cos she started growing distant right when I thought without a doubt that I was going to marry her. She started telling me I was predictable, a phony engineering major, a man who had no guts. She actually said I was no man at all."

"And I'm guessing that's the part that hurt the most?"

"Yeah," he said, looking down, clearly embarrassed at having revealed his discomfort so easily. She knew what to do.

"Happens to a lot of guys," she said, and she spoke from work experience. Girls seemed to want guys that could fix all their problems, with their muscly arms and pure brawn, or in this case, brains. There was no such man.

Ben looked up at Alexandra, and she smiled at him, what she hoped was an inviting, sympathetic smile. Clearly, it did the trick, for he uncrossed his arms and looked at the dirty dishes, thinking. "I'm guessing they all feel like complete numbskulls. For falling for a girl like that."

"Yes, I call them superficial girls, ones that don't care for what's inside, and only seem to see the outside, what can be done for them. They break a lot of hearts and must be evaded at all costs."

"The worst part is that she didn't break up with me," he told his sister. "She... well, she made me break up with her. Not really. I mean, she started treating me like a friend, even when I tried to explain to her why I wasn't exactly what she wanted, but could be, and she just, well, she threw me aside without even telling me that's what she wanted. I broke up with her when I realized I had spent a week without a proper text from her, over the break. She texted, but all of it was shallow, when we had used to have good, deep conversation in the beginning of our dating. I missed that and I missed her."

"You missed the *idea* of her, brother. You dodged a bullet. Those types of girls just want to use you."

Ben shuffled his feet, standing with his weight on one foot, then the other. "Probably." He looked at her and said, blank-faced, "Is this the part where I pay you for your help?"

She threw his pillow at him. "You get the family discount, no charge."

He caught the pillow and gave a short bow. "Thank you, Queen Alexandra, for your wisdom and listening ears."

"Be at ease, servant," she said, laughter tugging at her lips. Ben did the unexpected. He smiled, he grinned, and he broke into a fit of laughter. He doubled over, and she joined in, though a little wary of his reaction.

"Here I'm talking," he said between laughter, "about some stupid girl you don't even know the name of." He chuckled. "And you're listening with such patience that it doesn't even seem like you." He put a hand up, in apology, "I mean the you that used to rule the land at home, shutting everyone up with her oh-so-grand wisdom, thinking herself better than everyone."

"I do protest! I did no such thing."

"Yes, yes you did. You were bossy."

She giggled. "Okay, maybe a little."

"Dad used to hate it."

"Yes, but I stopped being like that after—" She stopped

herself midsentence to think about what she would say next, what she almost mentioned: the big elephant that was wedged in a corner of the room and looked at her with sorrowful, unforgiving eyes.

Ben stopped his merriment and looked down, rubbing his eyes. He seemed to never have ceased to notice the elephant, like she had. Maybe he saw it not as being wedged in a corner, but front and center, standing between them with a loud trumpet call, furious and unrelenting. He walked around the table, put fingers on it to steady himself (and she now noticed that somehow, it had stopped being rickety), and sat beside her.

"Let's go back to *Comatose*," he said.

"Tell me," she started.

"Hm?"

"When did you wedge that old notebook under the rickety leg of my table?"

"When I couldn't put my stuff down on it without getting irritated?"

She recognized that notebook. It had been *hers*. But she said nothing, for she knew better.

She smiled instead. "*Comatose*," she said.

***

Ben didn't want to talk about it. And so, he didn't. That's how it had always worked for him. Ignore it, and the hurt goes away. The hurt about Chelsea, his engineering girlfriend, had left just like that. It helped to talk about it now, yes, but he had two years of college to forget about it. He had used them wisely. He didn't graduate top of his class for nothing. Studying had become everything to him. When he had finished high school, he couldn't wait to enter college, to be away from it all. Now he was back, and Alex was hitting all the wrong buttons.

She didn't mean to harm him, he knew. But he had almost shed a tear, and he would not allow himself to. He rubbed his eyes, rubbing the budding tears away, and almost lost his balance getting back to the couch. Alex had surely noticed his fumble, but she didn't mention it. They talked about the table and that was that. They walked away from that subject, for they didn't need it.

Comatose had come as a balm, as a distraction. It had almost become the opposite and he didn't like it. But there was no way he wasn't finishing the game. He was glad when his twin sister agreed to go back to it. It was better this way.

Chapter 7

"What next, what next..." Alexandra murmured to herself, purposefully ignoring her brother, who was collecting himself on the seat beside her. "Ah! The bar. We had a memory awaiting us there." She picked up the microphone, ready to talk Jack into submission.

"How do you know we need to go back to the bar?"

"Because, dear sir, I skipped a memory snippet from there. On purpose. I didn't tell you. Pardon me."

"Hey, you said no pity, no judgment. Same here." He sounded better, so she looked at him. No tears, no runny nose, no red face, done and done. She hadn't broken him just yet, but if she pushed any further now, she was afraid he would crack. It was only day two, and she couldn't be having a broken boy to take care of just yet, so she let him be.

"Where was it?" he said.

"The memory snippet?" she asked, confused.

"Yes," he replied curtly.

She needed to focus, so she dispelled all thoughts of broken Ben away and got ready to work with whole Ben. Not whole; chipped. Whatever a sane person would call this stage of the problem. Chipped Ben was waiting for an answer, and Queen Alexandra was ready to give one.

"In the entrance of the bar. It was like a hiccup in his steps when he moved into it, and so I pushed him through, afraid we would have a hard reset yet again."

"Ah, yes, I remember now," he nodded.

One hand firm on the microphone, the other resting on the mouse she had placed on the notebook on her lap, she spoke. "Go back to the bar, Jack."

He obeyed, with no qualms, and she couldn't help thinking he was a tricky sort. He walked as if he were a little lost, and he stumbled a little while passing by a hillside, stopped for a moment, blinked, and kept on walking.

"Wait!" she shouted at Jack.

"Whoa," said Ben, startled. He had been looking at his screen. "Little warning next time?"

"Sorry," she said quickly. "Jack," she said clearly and sharply, "what is it?" Jack stood still and looked slightly over his shoulder, to the hillside.

"Do you want us to go there?" she asked, feeling a little silly for saying such a thing to a videogame character.

As response, Jack turned and faced the hill. "Walk toward it," Alexandra said, and he did.

As he reached it, the sun overhead shone brighter until the screen went white. Jack blinked it away, and it went to a nice cool day, when one could imagine a breeze picking up the grassy hillside. A girl who she presumed to be Kat could be seen sitting down on the grass, beside Jack's point of view. Jack said as the words sprung up on the screen, *She finally turned to face me, green eyeshadow ablaze.*

"New hallway!" Ben said, just as Jack shook his head and blinked, making Kat disappear like mist, and the whole of Solstice went back to its familiar, dusty self; the grass looked dead.

Alexandra looked over to Ben. Sure enough, he was walking into a hallway to the right of all the other ones they had unblocked until now. It was the first on that side of the corridor, and she wondered at this discrepancy. Ben pulled down the red book that was a little farther up than his character could reach without hovering higher with W. The trusty fountain pen appeared on the screen, and the book presented its spine to him. He typed in *Hillside* and the book opened.

"Did you do that?" Alexandra asked, quizzically.

"It opened by itself," Ben replied without much thought.

He typed in *Face me, eyeshadow ablaze*, and the sentence filled itself in. "How can eyeshadow be ablaze?" he asked no one in particular.

"Your guess is as good as mine."

"I think it means she's unhappy."

"Quite probably." Alexandra got out of her cross-legged position and put her socked feet on the floor. "She had eyeshadow on, so she must be older than the *Playground* memory."

"You could be onto something. Do continue."

"Sadly, that's all I've got. It must be close to the *Bar 2* memory, but why is it so distant from it? On a different side?" She put a fist against her cheek, elbow on a leg.

"We need to put the memories in order," Ben said.

"Now that I think about it, that must certainly be it," Alexandra concluded. "But we're still missing six years."

"Jack is missing them, not Kat."

"Correct."

"But their friendship before college is missing."

"Correct again."

Ben stood up. "We're missing things."

"Indeed we are."

"The question is where."

"Right again."

114

"Dang," Ben said, exasperated.

"Indeed."

"Welp," he announced, "let's try to get this hillside memory, and we go from there."

"One question, Benjamin," she said.

"Yeah?"

"Did the college or bar memory appear in the *Kat* book?"

"Nope."

"But we have the first memory in it."

"Yup."

"And the book for it is in the second hallway… Please go back to it." Ben did so with the arrow keys, and Alexandra confirmed her query. "Yes! It named itself *Playground 1*, so it must be the first memory."

Ben caught on. "Or maybe the first playground one," he said.

"So, the memories must only slot themselves in when we have them in the right order," Alexandra completed her thought.

"Sounds about right."

"I need to think," Alexandra said, a little flabbergasted.

"By all means. I'll take him to the coffee shop, see if we can find some green eyeshadow."

Alexandra hardly registered his words. She took the laptop and handed him the microphone and mouse.

***

Ben sat and took the microphone from his sister's limp hand. "Just me and you, Jack," he said, quietly. "Don't let me down this time." He stood very still on alert in case Jack suddenly reacted to his words onscreen. He did not. Ben breathed relief. So, he wasn't all ears after all. "Go to *Tom's Café*," Ben said into the mic. There he was, trying to find something to help him retrieve a memory by going to the coffee shop again. This game was getting repetitive. Then again, so was the last game he played, *The Cauliflower of Doom.* Maybe that was just how games were. Either way, Jack obeyed easily. When he had reached the coffee shop, Ben told him to go through the dusty door, and looked around with the mouse. He half-noticed Alex walking down an old hallway of books with the arrow and WASD keys, picking a red spine off the shelf. In the coffee shop were tables, the big teddy bear, the painting on the wall, and a whole lot of other stuff. How was he meant to find green eyeshadow in this crowded lost and found? He wasn't even sure he knew what eyeshadow looked like.

"Look for Kat's eyeshadow?" Ben asked Jack, very unsure of himself.

Jack took a step forward and looked around some more from where he stood, on his own. It seemed like he didn't know what it looked like either. Ben sighed frustration. "Walk to the nearest table," Ben said. Jack did. "Look through the objects for some makeup." Maybe this new tactic might work.

Jack rummaged through what was on the table with his sunburnt hands, taking a closer look at trinkets like a pair-less earring and what looked like a school paper of about ten pages. There was even a cushion on the coffee shop table, hiding an animal's food bowl. When Jack was done looking through the table, he stopped. He was awaiting a command. By this point, Alex had stopped what she was doing, too. Ben had two people waiting for him to do something right. The pressure was a little stifling.

"Next table," Ben said to Jack. He rummaged around again and came up with nothing. "Last table?" Ben asked, feeling a little hopeless. This time, Jack did not disappoint. He found a makeup kit by a high-heeled shoe. The moment he touched it; the screen turned darker until they could hardly see Jack's hands. The green hillside of before emerged from the shadows and Jack was transported. Kat was standing up, confronting him.

Toying with people's lives is not 'fun,' Kat, it's cruel, Jack said, reading off the TV screen. Anger was in his voice. The screen went black again, as Jack collapsed to the floor of the coffee shop. His breathing was quick.

"Calm down, dude," Ben comforted him. "Deep breaths." The TV screen settled into the legs of the table where they had found Kat's makeup. "Stand up," Ben said, encouraging. He sighed as Jack stood, steady on his legs. "Caught all that, Alex?"

She shoved the laptop into his hands. He had called her Alex again. He couldn't recall when she had started to dislike the nickname. The hillside memory was now called *Hillside 1* – at least the game liked helping them a little – and the words Jack had spoken were under the previous sentence Ben had put in. Excellent.

"Back to the hillside?" he asked Alex. But Jack replied first. The character had turned around and was walking out of the hole in the coffee shop's wall, as if it were a regular shortcut.

"Damn you, Jack," Ben muttered to himself. Alex chuckled beside him. "What, that's still creepy!" he said in protest.

"It isn't creepy to me anymore. I've gotten quite fond of it."

Ben smiled small. "What had you been up to while I failed to find a little thing of eyeshadow?" he asked. Ben popped a yellow Sweet Tart into his mouth. His tower was dwindling faster than he expected. His sister had probably been sneakily eating some. That made him smile a little bit more. But he contained himself and put on a sufficiently straight face.

"I've been looking over the memories we already have, and I've come up with some thoughts," his sister replied.

"Feel free to enlighten the rest of us." Ben splayed out his hands, palms up. He put them down as he let Alex collect her thoughts.

"Those cereal dishes are getting on my last nerve," she said suddenly. "I need to wash them."

"Come on!" Ben groaned.

"Patience, dear brother, is a virtue. One must learn to exercise it."

"Fine." He pursed his lips and picked up his dish. "You tell me while we wash the dishes."

"A compromise! I do like those. Come hither!" she said with glee, leading the way to the kitchen. Her red bowl and dirtied spoon were in her hand. She discarded them by the sink. The smell of burnt lobster was almost gone. Almost. Ben handed her his blue bowl, spoon sitting neatly in it.

"Is this it?" he asked her.

"I didn't have to make the cereal with a pan, you know that."

"Then I'll wash. You do the talking." Ben picked up a green-and-yellow sponge before Alex could do so.

"We know that Kat has been drinking ever since she was a teenager," Alex said. "I'm guessing probably fifteen or sixteen years of tender age. Jack doesn't like to drink, or at least he didn't when they first met. I'm still unsure about how much he drinks in the future because of her influence, and that is something I hope gets clarified. He prefers a latte for now, as far as we know from the right order of things. We are missing the continuation of their friendship that started in the playground that night and possibly budded into something more later on, but not entirely something. It seems to me, looking over everything we have at our disposal, that Jack clearly has a crush on her, ever since they first met. She, however, does not necessarily feel the same, although she did reveal some interest when drunk at the bar. Maybe the fight we are about to witness at the hillside is a lover's quarrel, and for some reason Jack wanted us to listen into it. Yes, yes, I know you are a skeptical man, but I think the game-makers made Jack very capable of thinking for himself. I was made aware of that when he first ignored one of my deliberate orders, just yesterday."

Ben had finished putting the last spoon away on the pink dryer by the sink. It stood in the way of Napoleon's fall into the watery abyss. Ben shook his head. "A lot of info, but I don't think you missed anything. Other than that, we are expected to be mediums and know where each memory should go."

"Context clues, brother. Context clues," she said, taking a drying towel from its hook by the bust. "We are missing data, however, so putting things in order is not our priority just yet." She started to slowly dry the dishes, making sure they were as dry as the deserts of Solstice.

"All right," Ben said, "let me look at those context clues."

***

Alexandra was drying the dishes slowly with a purpose. "Go, brother," she thought, "go get enrapt in the game as much as I am! Let it distract you a little while longer." She had already gotten past a milestone, the story of his failed relationship. She had no doubt Jack had heard the same words she had and wanted to furnish them with his own, for she had read longing as he stopped by the hillside, walking away from it with some sorrow in his eyes. Of course, she could never be sure of such a thing.

Maybe she was just being silly, but with every new memory, Jack felt like a real, breathing, living person to her. She welcomed the surprise of such an unknown game being so masterfully made, and wondered why there were not more copies out there. But that was a road sure to dead-end, so she forced herself to ignore it for now.

Jack needed them. She absently put away the last dish and walked with a spring in her step toward the sofa, Ben already in his spot, reading from the computer screen. Jack stood quite still outside of the café. He glanced around once, getting restless but keeping patience close at hand.

"May I?" she asked Ben, for she noticed the character hadn't started walking, even after he unpaused the game – she had paused it precisely after Jack had unceremoniously walked out of the café. She beckoned for the microphone with an open hand but realized Ben wasn't listening, so she took it from his lap herself.

He was engrossed in reading the latest memory they had found. "He must like her a lot," Ben concluded and slid down to the floor, laptop in hand, making sure Alexandra could still hold onto the microphone unhindered. He opted to put the laptop on his crossed legs, jeans a startling blue against its paleness.

"Go back to the hillside," she told Jack, but he did something curious, yet again, not surprising her at all. He balked and wouldn't move, and she knew she would have to coax the story out of him, just as she had done with Ben. Confident about her skills, she started speaking to him. "I know you're in pain, but I just want to help," she told the character on the TV screen. "If you let me, I'm sure I'll be a ready ear. But you need to accept to get through this." Jack took a hesitant step forward, gaze focused on his dusty, dark jeaned legs and the overwhelming dust that choked the ground from springing any life into it.

"I can't," Jack said, hardly above a whisper.

"You haven't even tried," she told him, firm.

The screen went foggy for a second from what she imagined were tears, but Jack quickly blinked those away, like a war-ready soldier. He started walking toward the dead hillside in Solstice, a place he had just barely kept from calling his own personal hell. When he reached it, the screen went black again, and yet he stood his ground, for the scene started to play out before them, Kat's long, wavy hair in his sights, for she had her back turned toward them. Alexandra beamed a little with pride for Jack and quickly had to push it aside to listen.

***

I was surprised she had answered my text and agreed to meet. She had ignored my call earlier in the day, like she was avoiding me. It had to be her. It couldn't have been anyone else.

"Got your message," said Kat, curtly. She was seated on the hillside, legs in dark jeans and drawn up. She was almost a silhouette in the pink setting sun. I could smell the faintest hint of alcohol wafting from her. She wore a maroon three-quarter shirt. "What is it? Need a drink?" Kat asked. She hadn't turned to look at me, but I knew she was getting impatient. "You didn't mention it, so I didn't bring one," she added.

My mouth went agape. "How can you be so nonchalant?" I said, angry and exasperated. "You just ruined a relationship and broke a man's heart!" I held up one of the flyers she had posted all around campus. It said, 'Slut lost.' Underneath it was Brittany's Facebook profile picture. Under that was 'If found contact: James, Spencer, Ian, Gabriel, Carter, etc.'

"Chill, Romeo, it can't be traced to me." She spat out a piece

of grass and picked another one. *"I used someone else's username on the library computer and was all secret-like."*

"That's not the point here, Kat." I thought I could trust her. *"You posted it all over school. Everyone was sending her death glares."*

"I wish I had brought a drink for me," Kat muttered under her breath. She finally turned to face me, green eyeshadow ablaze. *"Look, dumb fuck, she had it coming. He was bound to find out. I just expedited the process."*

"It was none of your business!" I stood in front of her so I could look her straight into those dark, menacing eyes.

"Didn't you think it was funny?" Kat stood up. *"No... 'cos you're more fun when you've had a drink. A little ball of anger and gossip. You don't like her even when you're sober. So why not appreciate a bit of fun, huh, Jack?"* she finished with jazz hands.

"Toying with people's lives is not 'fun,' Kat, it's cruel." I went further down the hill to look at her full in the face. This was beyond cruel – it was almost sociopathic. *"Carter looks the most depressed I've ever seen him."*

Kat scoffed. *"More depressed than when he got his first F in high school?"*

"You're not listening. You shouldn't do stuff like that to your friend's friends. You've humiliated them."

"Then people shouldn't let down the ones they love." Kat was visibly upset. *"You know what?"* she said. *"Fuck off."* She pushed me, almost strong enough to send me rolling down the hill and into the wire fence below. But I was quick and managed to keep my balance. She stormed off.

***

In the blink of an eye, Jack was tumbling down the dead-looking hill and hit the wire fence below with his feet, stopping himself from getting hurt. His breathing came quickly, as if he had run out of breath, out of will, out of everything. "Breathe," Alexandra told him. "Don't think, just breathe."

"She wasn't always like this," Jack told them, in between huffs of breath. "Something happened to her. I couldn't stop it."

"I understand," said Alexandra, not understanding much at all, but it seemed to do the trick. "Where was she when she was better?" she tried, not sure if her plan would work.

Jack stood up and looked ahead, breathing easy, now. Was it just her wishful thinking, or was Jack looking at the abandoned, sun-soaked playground beyond the wire fence?

"Is that—" Ben asked her without asking.

"The playground, yes, I think we must've missed something."

But Jack looked into the distance, to what looked like the small silhouette of the college building they had already found a memory in. She thought this odd, but wasn't about to question Jack now that she had gained his trust. The playground held answers, but he wasn't ready for those yet, it would seem like. She would have to leave her curiosity for later.

"Not the playground then?" Ben asked, a little confused. Alexandra looked at her brother's mysterious eyes, then looked away, at the computer screen.

"I don't think so, no. Not yet, anyways." Alexandra stopped talking, for she felt her stomach empty, as if she hadn't just eaten a bowl of sugary cereal. Suspicious, she looked at the bicycle-wheel clock hanging over the entrance to the kitchen. "Oh, dear," she said. "I am a terrible host. Lunch was supposed to be ready half an hour ago." She handed her brother the microphone. "Patience," she reiterated. "I don't like doing things on a grumbling stomach."

"I'm hungry, too, now that you mention it," Ben had to agree, and he pressed ENTER on the keyboard. Both screens paused, and he stood up, supporting himself on the couch behind him. "Need help?" he asked.

Alexandra stopped in her tracks – had he really asked her if she needed help? She knew he hated cooking, learned it early when their mother had tried teaching them the day after they turned thirteen. He had stormed off in the middle of the first lesson, clearly not enjoying it, and their mother had pleaded with him to come back. Yes, pleaded, guilt-tripping him, for that was how their mother was. She didn't want to dwell on the thought. "Only if you so wish," she finally told Ben, talking to him over her shoulder. Surprised, she heard his ready footsteps coming up behind her, and waited by the stove for him to catch up. He had never offered to help the last times he had shortly visited her, on some of his breaks from college, and she couldn't help but feel that her brother was growing up.

***

The female voice is kind. She guides me around this dead town with ease. Around finding her *once again, around her fury and her sweetness. She knows the right words to say to make me open up about things I wasn't even aware I was hiding myself. The boy is more lost, and I don't think he truly understands what is happening with me, with this place, with her. We try to find her eyeshadow together. Clumsy, is what I call it. But we only came closer to her wrath, and I am not ready for it.*

I should be, for it was so, so long ago, it seems. Why am I still hesitant? Why can't I keep away? Why must I love her so?

***

Alex was waiting for him by the stove, but she held nothing.

"Is the food gonna materialize for us?" he asked her, a little irked.

"We do tend to wish so when we are before the task of cooking, but sadly, no." She turned to face him. "How do mashed potatoes, meatballs, and broccoli sound?"

"Don't meatballs and mashed potatoes take long?"

"Not," she put up a finger, "if the mashed potatoes are from a bag and the meatballs are frozen."

"I used to do that with hamburgers."

"Quite," she said, smiling. In a flash, she took the bag of mashed potatoes from the pantry. "Try the fridge for milk and butter," she told him. "I'm sure you have already guessed where the broccoli and meatballs are."

Ben had learned to cook when he was forced to, sharing a flat with a few roommates while in college. His mother had tried teaching him, but he had refused to listen. He paid the price with a year of expensive store-bought food. Only then did he muster the courage to pick up cooking. That seemed to be the only way he ever learned: falling on his face. Now he was going to learn how to make this meal from his flurrying sister. He knew all about pre-made foods.

Bring it on.

***

125

Ben was apt in the bowels of a kitchen. Their mother had babied them when teaching them the trade, which is why her brother had stormed out of many failed cooking attempts with them both. Alexandra was different, for she knew her twin was capable of guiding himself. Soon, lunch was ready, and her brother looked happy with himself, which was a result Alexandra had not expected, but welcomed warmly.

"We make a pretty good team," she told Ben, while they sat on the sofa to eat. She had cleared the table from everything but his tower of Sweet Tarts (not before stealing a red one from under his very eyes) and put it all under the no-longer-rickety table. They put their feet up on the table and ate, the way hungry men who hadn't eaten in a while appreciated a good, semi-home-cooked meal.

Satisfied, Alexandra leapt to the kitchen in three strides, both plates – each delicate in its own way and bought from different thrift stores – and a pair of knives and forks in hand. She put them to soak, and yelled to Ben from the sink, "Would you like some cake?"

"Chocolate?" he yelled back.

"Yes sir, coming right up!" Alexandra replied and soon they were eating dessert off matching, intricately ornate little cake plates. They were one of her most prized possessions and she placed her empty plate carefully on the table, her feet back on the floor. Ben followed suit.

"Where were we?" Alexandra asked, truly lost. For her, a meal was an all-mind affair, a thought she had inherited from her mother.

"College and then playground?" Ben asked, and he was licking his lips, hoping to find any last vestiges of chocolatey goodness. There were none.

Alexandra nudged the laptop closer to his side of the room with a white-socked foot, and she smoothed her skirt with her hands. Ben obliged and picked it up, while she put a hand out for the microphone.

"Ready to go?" she asked him, lips pursed.

"Ready," he replied.

Chapter 8

Alexandra spoke to Jack, tenderness naturally making its way into her voice. "Go to the art building," she told him, and he strode to it with what she could swear was a spring in his step. They were probably on the right track now, and she acknowledged that Jack hadn't blacked out in a while. She let this thought make its home in her brain and smiled, for she was coming to know this new friend of hers, virtual or not. All he seemed to need was time, like her brother needed.

She tried to give them ample space, but she liked poking a short stick at them from time to time. So, she asked Jack, "Do you like the art building?"

Jack halted in his stride for a moment and said a resounding "Yes" before walking some more and stopping at the front steps of the towering, dead building. He was waiting for her guidance, and she looked at Ben.

"What's your plan?" he asked his sister. "The front steps are over."

"I do believe we heard Kat mention her art room to him. She even invited him to it. He must know the way. Go to Kat's studio." But Jack took a single step up the building's steps and stopped.

She commanded him to go into the bleak building, where everything seemed to be in ruins. Doors leaned precariously from their hinges. Walls were eaten into by what must have been a miniature wrecking ball: it did not destroy the walls completely.

She told him to go up the stairs and search for the room they were after. Even though he seemed uncertain, nothing seemed to stop him now. He looked here and there like he was entering into a place where he was a mere foreigner instead of a guest. He arrived at the end of a hallway flanked by rooms that looked like they were lit from the inside by some unknown source. He turned right, into the last room. It had been emptied in a hurry. A chair was on its side on the floor. An easel – which was clearly on its way to the floor – leaned empty against a wall. Placed neatly on the far wall was a black-and-white painting of a boy, somewhere in his mid-twenties. Ignoring all else, Jack made his way to it and touched its surface gingerly.

"This looks wrong," Jack voiced to no one in particular. "Where—" he was about to ask, but the painting emanated light where he had touched it. They all stared at it – Jack, Alexandra, Ben – as the light swallowed Jack's hand, his arm, his eyes, in a blinding gesture. The studio filled itself with art and color, and Kat stood in the midst of it all, empress and owner of a collection of paint, paintbrushes, easels, and paintings, working on one of them, back to Jack.

They were all abstract, but visually stunning, Jack thought, not wanting to perturb the master at work.

Alexandra looked at Ben, who was now looking at his computer screen, the laptop's keyboard under his poised fingers, ready and eager. He walked around until he found a new hallway waiting for him to the right. Somehow, this corridor seemed emptier than the others, and Alexandra didn't have to wrack her mind to figure out why. It had some empty places where faded books should be, but one of the books present was the red one they were there for, and so she didn't comment on it to her brother.

"This bookcase looks half-empty," he said.

"Yes, but there's the red spine we are looking for," Alexandra intervened.

"I have a bad feeling about this," and it certainly showed on his face. His mouth was slightly open, and his mismatched eyes were distant. "I don't know why," he said. "No matter, then, where is my trusty pen?" Ben moved his character down to the floor, to pry the shiny red book out of its spot, flanked by a drab black book on one side and a once-white one on the other.

The fountain pen appeared, and he wrote in *College 2* on its waiting spine, then *abstract, stunning* in the first line of the middle of the open book, the sentence fitting itself in like always. Finished, he looked up, and Alexandra only followed his gaze when Ben said, "Hey, where did it go?"

He was referring to the painting in Kat's studio. Jack was looking at an empty wall and he was shaking his head slowly.

"Do you remember seeing some paintings, just like Jack mentioned, in the café?" Alexandra asked, excited, for she knew just what they needed to do.

"They looked kinda dusty, but yeah, I think we can call them stunning," Ben replied. Jack was already on his way down the stairs, reaching the first floor with heavy breaths. "Wait," Alexandra pleaded into the microphone. "Wait for us, Jack." Jack stopped abruptly, but he looked intently toward the exit of the building.

"Okay," Jack said plainly.

Alexandra guided him back to *Tom's Café*, voice calm and steady, and Jack himself became calmer with her guidance. He walked through the front of the place and stood, patient.

"Pick up any paintings you can find," Alexandra said, firm, and Jack went about his work. He found the one on the counter, an abstract of red, and reached his arm out to touch it. He blinked and read from the screen, *Another was a red gash, darker around the edges.* He blinked, and the painting had disappeared.

"Write that down, please," Alexandra told Ben, and didn't look to see if he obeyed. "Do you remember seeing another?" she asked Jack.

In reply, Jack walked toward one he had missed closer to the entrance of the building. He described this one too before it disappeared. *One was a mix of blues and yellows, bordering on gold.*

"There was one more, Jack," she encouraged him, "on the wall?" Jack hesitated but found it without much trouble.

Yet another was blacks and greys sprinkled on the canvas. This one vanished as well.

"Is that it?" Ben asked and Alexandra had almost forgotten about him. She glanced at him now.

"Yes, I think so," she said. Jack didn't argue, so she had to assume she was right. "To Kat's studio!" she said with glee and off they went. Ben chuckled beside her, and she pretended to ignore it. She put the tip of her tongue out, focused on Jack's progress. She felt like she was witnessing the thrill of the chase, for he was almost running, and soon he was in the studio once more. The paintings had transferred to it and all three of them were in their proper places in the little room. The one of the boy had not yet returned home, and she thought this rather odd.

"Hey, my hallway just got fuller," Ben said with a hint of confusion in his voice.

"Naturally," she dismissed him with her free hand. She was clutching the microphone with the other and ordered Jack. "Touch the blue and gold painting," she said, and he did. Light erupted from his fingers yet again and this time the scene they

131

were expecting eagerly played out, Jack narrating with a voice that was almost a whisper. It grew louder as he read on.

***

Kat had texted me to come to her studio area. This was the first communication she had attempted since she had tried pushing me into a wire fence. I took her humbly-worded text as an apology and accepted it. I found her room and sidled in.

Her studio was spacious but felt cramped. Kat had incomplete canvases, paints, paintbrushes, and sketches on every possible surface. She had her finished projects on the walls. They were all abstract, but visually stunning. One was a mix of blues and yellows, bordering on gold. They swirled around each other like a whirlwind in a sun-bathed sea. Another was a red gash, darker around the edges. Yet another was blacks and greys sprinkled on the canvas, but I could tell where she had smudged some of it to look like dirty rain on a pavement. None of them bore titles.

"Where are their names?" I asked sheepishly. I remembered that day when we had discussed art in the treehouse. I hoped I wasn't opening an old wound.

Kat shook her head. "There you go, always searching for the words," she said with a sigh. "Haven't changed, have you?"

"I don't..." I started to say. No. She wasn't a teenager anymore. "I still think a piece of art lacks meaning if it's untitled," I said. "That's what I was trying to say all those years ago."

"Jack found his mojo, huh," she scoffed. She sipped at a glass of wine. I had no idea where it materialized from. She saw that my gaze was fixed on it. "Relax," she said, "I only ever drink

the one."

"What happens if you drink more?"

"You know..." she mused, "I start talking to my art pieces." I must've looked unsettled because she continued. "I'm kidding, dummy," Kat said. "If you must know, I lose my sense of focus and start wanting to make everything look all bright and yellow."

"Is that what happened with this one?" I asked and pointed to the blue and yellow canvas.

"No," she said, nodding at it like she was thinking it over, "that was on purpose."

"Oh," I said, disappointed.

"I call it 'Restless Rain,' in case you were wondering."

"Ah," I said, studying it closer. "Glad you've followed my advice and gave them words."

"I never really disagreed with you," she said. "I think an art piece at least needs a title that will give it meaning." I looked at her and she was grinning. "Did you think all this time that I was mad at you about that conversation?"

It was foolish of me to think she had been, but I did. "You gave a snarky remark and stormed off." Before she could come up with another snarky remark, I continued. "Is that what that red one is? Your response?"

She laughed her melodic laugh. "Almost," she said. She carefully picked the red canvas from off the wall. "I call this one 'The Drunkard,'" she said. She looked at it longingly for a moment and I thought she might tear up. But she placed the painting back to rest on its nail.

"And that one?" I asked to change the subject. "The grey one?"

"Well," she said, "I'm not done with that one yet."

"Oh." I looked away from it. "Thought you might be," I

said, letting the thought go.

"I'm not sure I will ever finish it," she murmured, more to herself than me.

I looked at her from where I stood beside her. The sad look on her face, the one I knew too well, was back. My hands were in my pockets because I didn't want to accidentally touch anything and get scolded. But now I wanted to reach out an arm and hold her, though I knew it was not the place, much less the time. Before I could decide on what to do, she had whirled around.

"I've got this wall, too," she said. "These are all finished." I looked behind me.

She was right. I had hardly seen that wall of paintings when I had walked in. These looked older. Their colors were not as sharp or their brush strokes as poignant. In some, if you looked closely enough through the confusion of colors, you could almost make out images.

"I made these earlier in college," she explained. "To vent, mostly." I could tell. She went down the row of them. The first one was a splash of dark blues and purples. "That one is called 'Bitter at 2,'" she said. The next one was browns slathered with red. "That's called 'Home Indeed,'" she said. "It took me a while to be satisfied with it." She drank the rest of her wine in one gulp. "The rest is unimportant," she said dismissively.

"Are you sending me away?" I asked.

"Wait, I forgot." Kat reached under her desk and started to pull out a canvas. "Close your eyes," she said. I did. "Okay, open them." I looked at what she presented me.

It was like looking into a black and white mirror. She had sketched a picture of me looking sideways and down. I had my missing octopus T-shirt on and sported a wide smile, like I was containing laughter. One of my hands was through my hair, arm cocked at an angle so you could still see my eyes. The detail in them was amazing. I could see the lines in my hazel irises – though these eyes were only a light grey. She had masterfully used shadow to make it look like the sun was about to set, though the canvas held no sun. Only me. I knew I made that pose when I laughed, but I had never consciously thought it through. She had made an art piece out of a moment that would now last forever.

"Stop gawking over it and take it home," Kat interjected. She returned my T-shirt and looked at an invisible watch on her wrist. "Visiting time is over," she said. "I have work to do."

She shooed me out of her studio. I was so stunned I didn't even give her a 'thank you.' I looked at the back of the canvas. It held one word as title: 'Coffee.'

***

The stifling air of the art studio faded with the scene and then the room was empty, save for the painting that had been there before – the one of Jack. It was covered in a thin layer of dust that he cleaned with an unsteady hand. He had crouched to reach the painting and when he finished, he stood and turned his back toward it.

"I am ready," he said with strength in his voice.

"For the playground?" Alexandra asked kindly, just as she had learned to do with her customers when they reached the end of their love stories. At this point, she usually suggested a flower for them to take home, to present to the person in question. They usually followed her suggestion.

"Yes," Jack said quietly.

Alexandra looked over at Ben, whose gaze was fixed on the television screen. He must've sensed her, for he said, "Jackpot?"

"Jackpot," she said with a nod.

***

"Wait a bit," Ben said. "Is it just me, or did Jack bring us a breakup story just as we had finished talking about ours?" The thought had been stuck in the back of his mind since Carter and Brittany's story. It was now first in his cluttered mind.

"Maybe Jack wanted to share," Alex said, getting more comfortable on the couch.

These memories were becoming a little too much for him. They came too close to his experiences. But he wasn't going to reveal that to his sister, no matter how patiently she waited. He could sense she was doing so and silently thanked her for it. He had almost mustered the nerve to tell her that her waiting game wasn't going to work. His heart was a safe with strong and sure locks.

He had his own questions for her, ones he never felt he had the right to ask. But since they were finally sharing with each other again, he thought she might open up. At least she would do so more easily than him. He wanted the bullseye away from him. This visit wasn't about him. It was never supposed to be. This visit was about having a place to stay until some solid job showed up. Then he would find someone to room with and a place to stay permanently. He hadn't made much progress in that area. In truth, he hadn't made much progress other than in *Comatose,* with his sister. He welcomed the distraction. But the game was turning into something else.

Why did she have to pick the game with the lifelike main character? Why did it have to be made of loose ends? And why did it have to involve love, a relationship? *The Cauliflower of*

Doom had been nothing like this. His sister *had* to find the drama game. And he found himself enjoying it, somehow. He felt useful. That was it. They were helping this man Jack find his way. They'd had a bumpy start, but now they had gotten the hang of it.

"Now, where to?" Alex broke into her brother's thoughts. Was she talking to Jack, or to him?

He glanced at her. She was looking at him. He turned his eyes to the computer screen, on his lap. "Uhm," he said, looking up, "hold on, you're already at the playground?"

"Yes," she said, "he went by himself."

"Let me check if I got a new hallway of books." He needed to focus. "Let me check," he repeated. "Aha!" he said, finding a new book-filled hall beside the last one they had found on the left.

This side of the corridor was almost full with lit hallways now. To the right, there were only two memories at the start of it. He frowned, and walked into the new hallway to the left, after the four hallways that were already there (the ones of Kat's house, the playground, the university steps, and the bar). The red book was before him. He walked to it and took it from its place on the shelf. "I didn't miss a snippet, did I?" He was already typing *Playground 2* on the spine.

"Not that I am aware of, brother," was Alex's reply. He thought she sounded cheeky. She was certainly grinning at him. He didn't dare look.

"What are you waiting for, dancer?" The last word had slipped off his tongue with some bite. He hadn't allowed it to leave in such a fashion. Yet it was loose. She had made the smallest, almost imperceptible movements in the kitchen, while mixing the potato powder into the milk.

She had had classical music on Spotify, and it was getting in the way of her cooking. He thought this was a good thing, and so he mentioned it. "Dancing again, are we?" he asked with a smile.

"No," she had replied. And from then on, she had stopped her swaying, deliberately. He had ignored her curt response and asked if they still needed the milk.

"Ben," she said. "About that," she continued. But she didn't look like she knew how to continue. Were tears springing in her eyes? He must be imagining it. She straightened her back into a plank, let go of the microphone. It lay haphazardly on her lap. She wiggled her toes once. Then steadied herself. "You know I stopped dancing."

"Why?" Ben crossed his arms across his chest, but not before pausing the game with the ENTER key.

"You know why," she said.

"You had a job lined up. Dance was your dream!" he said vehemently. "You threw it all away for a rose shop."

"I know that, Benjamin!" She was set to cry. "I think about it every week." He didn't want her to cry but she had sparked his curiosity.

"Every week?" he asked, loosening his grip on his arms. He hadn't noticed he had tensed his hands. He slacked his frame.

"Because Mom calls every week." Ben had not been aware of that. He regretted his comment now. "She's bound to call any minute," Alex continued. Ben braced himself for having possibly broken the dam. "Dad talks for maybe a minute every time when she passes the phone to him. He always sounds gruff." She looked down at her fidgeting hands. "But she asks me how I'm doing, what I've been up to, and she always asks me when I'll pick up my dancing again." She looked up at him quickly, then back down. "I always tell her sometime soon. I haven't had the heart to tell her I threw all my dance clothes away, my leotards, my skirts, my ballet shoes. She doesn't get it." She looked up at him again.

Her unasked question was 'Do you?' He looked at her, gaze steady. She had a tear rolling down her chin. He tightened his arms again. He didn't know how to stop what he had started. He didn't feel like joining in. It was an open wound. Slowly, gently, he wiped her tear away with a finger.

"Forget about it," he said. "Let's go back to the game." So they did. Ben unpaused the game.

"Jack," Alex said, and Ben was glad to hear it come out steadier. "Go to the sandbox." Jack walked toward it, stepped into it. Nothing.

"Maybe the treehouse?" Ben asked, joining his sister in the search.

Jack passed by the monkey bars, the seesaw, and arrived at the front of the treehouse. It was falling apart. He didn't go up the battered stairs, but his gaze was fixed on them.

"Go up them," Alex coaxed him on.

The moment Jack put a foot on the bottom step, the whole of the treehouse put itself back together. Wood arrived from the grass, the sandbox, all unseen a second before.

A young Jack and Kat were sitting in the treehouse, bodies close in the twilight.

To their surprise, Jack started narrating the memory without the need of writing in a snippet. They didn't even need to take a trip to the coffee shop for an item.

***

Kat and I met up every Wednesday at the playground after dusk.

She had told me that was the time of day her dad drank the most. Her mom hardly noticed her absence then, trying to keep her father quiet and satisfied. The warm drinks helped keep us busy on something other than our awkward teen selves. She had convinced me to stop caring about police cars and to 'live a little.' So sometimes we sat in the treehouse and talked. Other days we used the see-saw, the sandbox, or the monkey bars. She liked to hang upside down from the bars and try to keep her drink steady. She reminded me of a circus acrobat. I sat on the bars across from her and worried about her falling. She never did.

Some days she was a chatterbox about what happened at her school and the gossip floating around. Those days we sat in the grass beyond the grounds and talked. Other, rare days, she was morose and silent and preferred the swings. We swung on them standing up and I did the talking, though sparse. She never told me much about her family life, but I'm sure that was what upset her then. She told me her mom worked at a fancy restaurant as a hostess. Her dad was between jobs. She had a little brother who was a 'sweet pea.' That was all the information she was willing to give me.

But we talked about everything else there was to talk about and discussed a lot of what there was to discuss. I learned much about her; she was a nihilist that loved penguins and the color green. She also loved art. We disagreed on that last topic. I was all about the classics and held the belief that abstract art wasn't art. That day we were in the treehouse, legs crossed, knees almost touching.

"Jack," she said after she took a drink. "Art is about expressing what you feel. Feelings are abstract. Therefore," she concluded, "art has the right to be abstract." I sipped some of my latte and sat in silence for a few moments. "Think of

Beethoven," she continued when she noticed I had no counterarguments ready. She waved her arm in a grand gesture, as much as the structure of the treehouse would allow. "Or any other classical musician. There are no words."

"I'm not saying music can't be instrumental," I said and sipped the last of my drink. "I'm saying..." I squeezed the Styrofoam cup, trying to find what I meant to say.

"Yes?" she asked, impatient. She had her hands on her hips. I had the feeling she was testing me.

"I think we have different premises," I said finally. She huffed. "I think art is about expressing something toward an audience," I continued, unabated. "I think classical music is valid, but I don't get much from it." I looked down at the dirty wood to think more clearly. From the corner of my eye, I saw Kat cross her arms in defiance. "All I'm saying is that words help," I said, looking up. She was staring at me with those dark eyes that I could drown in. "Besides," I said, blinking, "the classics in music are extremely different from the classics in art. Paintings, I mean." She had to agree on that one.

"Well, yes," she relented and turned her death glare away. "They had sculptures and big, old paintings of people before abstract art came along." Kat was always touchier when it came to visual art. I shouldn't have brought it up, but it was inevitable; she had told me it was her form of expression. I had never seen one of her canvases or drawings, though she said she drew and painted almost constantly.

"Maybe you're a sour puss," she said, "and don't understand abstract art." Kat threw her empty Styrofoam cup to the trashcan below. It almost missed. "If you're a good artist, colors evoke all the emotions you need," she finished.

"They evoke different emotions in different people," I

141

objected. "That's why it doesn't work for me. It's subjective." I
tried making the shot into the trashcan. I did miss and had to go
down the slide to retrieve my cup. I heard her snicker above me.
She jumped off the treehouse with a low thump and was by my
side.

"You go home and write a poem about something that upsets
you," she said, "and I'll go home and make a blood-red canvas
expressing how angry I am about you not agreeing with me. Next
Wednesday we can compare notes."

"You know I can't write poetry," I protested. She tilted her
head back with finality and started walking away, to the fence. I
followed her. "Do I at least get to see this painting?" I asked. I
was hoping against chance for a 'yes.' Kat stopped in her tracks.

"Hm…" she said, just loud enough for me to hear. "Maybe."
She jumped over the fence in a graceful motion. I watched her
back as she strode around the bend, to the direction of home. She
always refused to let me walk her there. I had learned not to ask.

***

Jack was back in Solstice, just inside the playground.

Ben stared at the TV screen. Then he stared at the computer
screen. The book he was holding had filled its pages with the
scene. "We found it?" he gasped. "The second memory?"

"Yes!" Alex replied with glee. "Yes, we have!"

She was happy again, which made him happy. He allowed
himself a small smile. "All right," he said, "now we…"

"We put it in the right place in the memory palace!"

"Is that what we're calling it?"

"The term isn't the correct one, but it was the best one I could
find. Shall I?" she asked, ready to take the laptop from his hands.

"No," he said. "It's my honor, your highness."

This made his sister chuckle. With a smile he wasn't too aware of on his face, Ben did the honors. He walked outside the last hallway into the long one that held all the others. Not to his surprise, this time the book went with him. He went with it until the beginning of the hallway. He entered the third corridor to his right. He found the *Playground 2* spine that was already there before, and replaced it with the same titled book that his character held. The old book vanished before their eyes.

Ben looked up, worried, at Jack. But he betrayed no change other than a single blink. Ben sighed. "We're safe," he blurted out.

"Safe and sound," Alex said. "I was growing quite tense."

"So was I," Ben murmured.

"Perhaps the *College 1* book is already the third memory?"

Ben obliged, but the book would not leave its hallway with him. It slotted itself back into its place on the populated shelf. "Welp," he said. "We are dead-ended again."

"That's all right, brother dear, we have made enough progress already."

"Yup," he had to agree. "We sure did."

They were interrupted by Alex's smartphone. It was ringing from its place under the low table. Alex looked at the caller ID, and she went a shade pale. "Mother," Alex told Ben. "Sorry, I need to get this." Flustered, his sister threw the microphone to him and walked to the kitchen.

The phone was still ringing in her hand. She only picked up when she was out of Ben's sights.

Tricia

Tricia, her seven-year-old sister, was very convincing when she wanted to be, and this happened to be one of those days. Tricia really wanted to go to the river on a school-night – a Thursday.

"I have an important dance recital tomorrow, Trish," said Alexandra. "You know this full well. Don't come asking impossible things." She picked at her leotard, looking at herself in her wall-length mirror. She smoothed out her skirt but saw Tricia out of the corner of her eye, still in her room and persistent. "All right, shrimp, give me your arguments," she told her sister. The little girl had a determined look on her small face and in her stance, which made Alexandra almost chuckle. She refrained from doing so.

"I love seeing you dance perfectly," said Tricia, putting up a finger.

"Yes," Alexandra replied, not understanding the connection between dancing and the river.

"But I *also* love playing at the river with you and Ben and if you don't go it just won't be the same, Alex! It won't!" she pleaded with her voice and hands.

Ben popped his head in. "I heard my name," he said. "What y'all hiding?" He tried to sound disinterested but failed.

"She wants to dance instead of go to the river with us," said Tricia, pointing an accusing finger at her older sister.

Ben plopped himself on the indigo beanbag right inside Alexandra's room. "We're going to the river?"

Alexandra sighed. "It would seem so," she conceded.

"Awesome!" said Ben. He gave Tricia a not-so-secret secret wink. He took some Sweet Tarts out of his pocket and offered one to her.

"You were in on this?" Alexandra asked, arms crossed.

"Oops," said Ben, which made Tricia giggle behind her

hands. "What can I say," Ben continued, "I've been wanting to go fishing and she asked so nicely."

"No," said Alexandra, "I am *not* going to see you dig in the dirt for worms again."

"Aw, come on, Alex," Ben implored, face all drama and droopy eyes. He was thirteen and had no shame. "Pleeeease?"

Tricia looked at her brother and copied his face the best she could. "I won't give you a frog to touch," she told Alexandra. "I'll touch those."

"What would be my reward for going on this expedition?" Alexandra said, arms still crossed, clearly up for negotiation. "On a school night of all things," she said gravely, "with an important dance recital the next day?" She had practiced her dance too much already, but she wasn't about to say so.

"Hm..." Tricia thought hard for a second with her eyes closed. "A cricket! You can take it home in a little jar and keep it as a pet!" she said, excited. "I would," she mumbled.

"Doable," said Alexandra and she made a face like she was pondering the offer.

"Ben, can we explore the woods, too?" Tricia asked. The little girl was smart and knew Alexandra would've said no immediately. Ben was more malleable, but hopefully not on this.

"You've asked millions of times," Ben said, and he made a climactic pause. "The answer is still no." Alexandra let go of the breath she had held.

"Aaaaaw, but why?" Tricia asked.

"You know it's dangerous. There are snakes," the boy argued.

"It looks so peaceful!" She tried to reason with him, but she always failed.

"Even bears," he said with hands up like claws, teeth bared.

"There are no bears in this part of the country, Benjamin," said Alexandra. "Have you ever seen one?" She bent down to slip off one of her ballet shoes.

"Have you ever *not* seen one?" Ben glared.

"That's flawed logic," she said and took the second shoe off.

"Whose side are you on?" Ben asked, sitting up taller on the beanbag.

Tricia laughed. "That's 'cos she wants to go to the river with us."

"Aaaaaah," said Ben, "how astute of you." He high-fived the little girl and she smiled wide. "We've won."

"I'll take my sketchbook," Alexandra decided, "and draw Ben picking at dirt and finding nothing," she mocked. "It might be a bit of fun."

"It *always* is, you just don't like nature," said Tricia.

"Not this again…" Ben said. He stood between them. "Listen," he said, conspiratorially. "We have a few hours before dusk. Mom and Dad can't find out." Ben looked up in thought. "I don't remember where I put my fishing rod…"

"Fine," Alexandra said, "get out so I can change." Ben put his hands up, innocent of all wrongs, and left the room. Tricia started to run off, but Alexandra took her by the wrist. "You are not going in those shoes," she said. "Change them out to your sneakers." She let go of her sister.

"But I love these!" Tricia protested, displaying her foot so the dancer could see the pros of such a shoe. "They have glitter on them! That helps see in the dark."

"I don't mind that those are cute, and your sneakers aren't," Alexandra said harshly, but then she saw Tricia's expression go sad. "I just don't want you slipping again," she concluded, caressing the girl's long, wavy hair. "It was a bad scrape."

"Yeah…" said Tricia, "it really hurt." She put a smile on. "Okay!" she said, and ran off.

Alexandra shook her head in disbelief and took off her dance clothes. The fifteen-minute walk to the river wasn't bad, but she would have to do extra stretches beforehand.

Soon they were all ready and back in her room. Alexandra looked at them both. "Sun starts setting," she said, "we run home." Tricia nodded sagely.

"Mom and Dad in their office?" she asked Ben, and he nodded.

"All right, sir and madam," she put her hand out for Tricia to take, "it is sneaking time."

Chapter 9

Ben was worried for Alex. She had been pacing in the kitchen for about five minutes, speaking monosyllables into the phone. Had their parents known he was going to be there? Had Alex told them? They might've guessed. Or possibly ripped it out of her. Either way, he had a feeling the subject of conversation wasn't Alex this time around. She wasn't speaking enough for that to be the case. Was she being scolded? He could hardly see her face as she walked.

Suddenly Alex started talking a flood. She spoke quickly. She told their mother about how she finally took a break from work, how she was still loving it, how Benjamin was searching for jobs around town, how they were having a good time, how he had washed the dishes for her, had even helped her with lunch, and how she was going to meet up with a friend tomorrow to catch up. Yes, it was Andrea. Another yes. A moment of silence on Alex's part, and then she muttered a no. From where Ben sat, he saw Alex stop in her tracks. Tears were present in her voice. "Yes, mother," she was saying. "I'll think about it. Yes, I know. Okay. Bye."

Alex left her smartphone on the kitchen counter and came back to the living room. The usual spring in her step was gone. She sat, heavy, beside Ben on the couch. For some seconds she was listless. Ben didn't know what to do. So, he stayed beside her, present. Then he asked, "Is it like that every time?"

"Like what?" Alex asked.

"Like you're being interrogated by the Spanish Inquisition."

This brought the smallest of smiles from Alex. "Yes, mostly," she replied. "It's okay, they haven't executed me yet."

Their parents had paid for Ben's four years of college and had never spoke a word to him again. He always imagined that they felt obligated to pay for his higher education, as parents. Other than that, they kept their distance. He had learned to be glad for it. He didn't judge them, for he blamed himself, too.

Now he felt for his sister. What was worse, being ignored or being interrogated? Probably the second. Neither of them had ever had what could be called a good relationship with their parents. But they appeared to still care. They called Alex, didn't they? They talked about him through her, as if she were a messenger pigeon.

Right now, she didn't need any more dwelling on their parents. He decided on distraction. "Ready to find the next memory?" he asked her, finger ready on the keyboard.

"Yes," she said in a low voice he almost didn't hear. She still smiled, however. He took that as a good sign. Ben handed her the microphone.

"Carry on," he said.

Alex put on her thinking face. Her tongue stuck out slightly. "What we have," she started, "are some future memories. We are missing the ones in the middle. The ones that connect everything. Go to the *Hillside* memory, please," she told Ben. With little difficulty, he found it.

He reread it out loud for Alex. "How did they get to the pamphlet?" Alex wondered. "Why does it seem like she is blaming *him* for it? Why does it sound like she betrayed Jack? Carter is his friend, it seems, but not enough of one for him to tell Carter who made the pamphlet."

"That means his allegiance lies with Kat."

"It would seem so…" his sister said.

"He's friends enough to take her home after she got drunk at the bar," Ben put in.

"True. Get that memory for me next, please?"

Ben read it aloud. "I had almost forgotten about this unknown character named Max."

"Yes, I feel like when we find out who he is, a lot of things will clear up."

"And why is Jack turning her down?" Ben said in protest. "She wants something from him, and he won't even cuddle."

"Maybe their feelings for each other are a tad different."

"How?"

"I'm not entirely sure yet. I need more memories."

Ben smiled. "Then let's get some." His twin's thoughts had turned away from their parents, without a doubt. He internally patted himself on the back.

***

Alexandra was aware of what he was trying to do: distract her from the dreaded phone call with their parents. He didn't question her about it more than he deemed necessary, and she accepted this respite. She might cry if she talked about her mother's biting, demanding words, or her lack of interest for her own son other than to know if he was making money yet. She wanted to know if they were spending Ben's precious time on another one of those useless videogames. Alexandra had said no – it was actually a computer game, so it wasn't technically lying. Her mother had grown curious when Alexandra had mentioned Andrea, her fellow dancer and oldest friend. She demanded to know if Alexandra was going to let her friend change her mind and if she was finally going to go back to dance and let go of her petty job at a lowly flower shop. The job offer she had gotten right out of high school could still be rearranged; her mother assured her.

Alexandra had said her goodbye, had old wounds reopened, and gone straight to her brother, whether for comfort or something else was unclear to her. It just felt right, for they had been close, once. Therefore, the distraction he placed in front of her, as she had done before for him, was most welcome.

They talked about what they already knew and what still needed to be done in *Comatose*.

"Walk about the city slowly," she told Jack, her grip firm on the microphone. She noticed something she hadn't seen before; a smaller house tucked away down a meager, cobbled road. She remembered their earlier wondering in the game if Jack lived in Solstice. She had only seen the house this time because Jack's head turned to it as he walked past. "Walk to the house," Alexandra said before Jack had strolled past it entirely, and she was eager to know what was about to be unleashed.

He stood at the small house's corroded front steps, and as his hand reached for the door, he blinked. Everything went dark. The low sound of laughter could be heard as the house bloomed in front of them, windows lit, night dark, front door neatly in its place, closed.

Jack spoke as the words emerged on the screen: *The bottle she had used to knock on my front door at one in the morning was long gone.* Light erupted from the front door and the house was bathed in dust and sun yet again.

"New hallway to the right," Ben announced. Alexandra stared at the dusty front door's doorknob that remained unperturbed, as if it had never seen the night nor felt a hand turn it tentatively. Ben had written *House* on the newfound red spine. The word *Jack's* placed itself before it, and Alexandra momentarily felt a surge of triumph at her right guessing about whose house it was. But they had more pressing matters at hand than a small victory.

Ben talked to himself as he put the words on the page, *one in the morning.* The words gave way to the memory snippet, and Ben said, "Back to the bar, maybe?"

"Perhaps," Alexandra said, quite unsure, and she reached over to the small plates that were still on the table in front of them. She skipped to the kitchen with them, allowing the memories of her phone call with their mother to fade away as she washed them carefully with the soft, yellow side of the sponge. She heard Ben flush the toilet in the only bathroom. Drying the dishes with a soft towel she had taken from a drawer, she put the ornate plates on the shelf over the sink, where they belonged. Then they were both back in the living room, Ben on the floor, having pushed aside the things they had left under the table to make way for his legs. He handed her the microphone as she sat down behind him on the couch, legs crossed, knees touching her brother's back lightly, back straight. Ready.

"Go to the bar," Alexandra told Jack. He left his house, desolate and abandoned, and walked the short distance to the bar. To her surprise, Jack stopped on the front steps and as he crossed the threshold with one foot, he blinked twice, the screen went dark again and Kat was beside him, holding his hand. *I looked at the fake ID she had made me and was impressed at her seamless handiwork,* Jack read aloud, amusement in his young voice. He blinked and she was gone, daylight back in place. This had to be the memory she had overlooked, a new one.

"Where is the new hallway?" Alexandra asked her brother

and saw he was already searching for it. Their newfound hallway was between the one that held the playground memories and the college one. Soon enough, he had the memory snippet on the page in front of him.

"Should we look for a fake ID in the coffee shop?" Ben asked.

"We shall," Alexandra voiced, a little unsure of herself, for she couldn't decide whether they should pursue the bar memory or the one at Jack's house. They could always try completing both, she argued with herself (they would have to eventually). She walked Jack to *Tom's Café* and made him search for a fake ID. There was a green beer bottle on the counter, she noted, and when Jack refused to turn over objects to look for the ID under them, she had him pick up the bottle instead.

"He wasn't working hard enough to find the fake ID for the bar memory," she explained to Ben, and she was glad he understood, though it seemed to her like a flimsy argument. Jack picked up the bottle and blinked as *'This just gets better,' she said and sat back up,* appeared on the TV screen. He read it with a wariness in his voice and, unlike all the other times, the world in front of them didn't change to the setting of the memory snippet.

"That's odd," Ben said, voicing Alexandra's concern, "he usually blinks to the setting."

"Yes," she said in almost a whisper, and made a mental note that something was wrong about this entire affair. Ben just shrugged and put the words into the red book where they belonged. Alexandra watched his progress and couldn't help but think that the rest of the words of the snippet took their time emerging on-screen. She made a mental note of that, too.

"To Jack's house?" Ben said, apparently loud enough for Jack to hear, for he started walking from the café to his house on its meager street, not in a hurry. He was about to put his hand on the doorknob, deliberate, when he started blinking non-stop, breathing fast and anxious. Jack held his head in his hands and before Alexandra could tell him to breathe, both screens became overcome by white light and Jack was at sea.

"Swim!" she urged, and he swam back to Solstice. She looked down at the computer screen on Ben's lap, worried for his temper. Ben was walking down his main corridor and he did not look happy.

"All the hallways are gone!" he groaned. As soon as Jack was on land, in front of the cracked and dry water fountain of the sun-soaked city, Ben paused the game. He found Kat's book on the menu screen and opened it eagerly. It still had the two playground memories, and he heaved a staggered sigh of relief. He pressed ENTER and his corridor came back into view.

"There's the first red book hallway still," Alexandra said reassuringly, but not reassuring enough for Benjamin.

"Do we have to do it all over again?" Ben looked up, neck strained to see his sister behind him, clearly failing but accepting of this failure.

Alexandra reached over and patted him on the shoulder. "Let us hope not."

Ben looked back down to the laptop screen. He let out a short sigh and said, "I quit. For now. I just… I quit!" He put the laptop on the table, almost startling his small tower of Sweet Tarts out of place, and got up in haste. He walked over to the TV screen and said, pointing at Jack's point of view, "You just had to ruin it for us, didn't you, buddy."

Jack blinked as if in reply and shook his head once, saying, but not saying, "Hey, you made me."

"I did *not* say that close enough to the microphone for him to react," Ben told his sister, turned in her direction, finger now pointing to the mic still in her hand. "This *game!*" he said, exasperated, his hands up above his head.

"Has it soured your good moods?" Alexandra asked sheepishly, not wanting to entice her brother more. His mismatched eyes were ablaze in latent fury and her thoughts cowered before it. She hadn't reacted fast enough, so the reset was as much her fault as Jack's, or even her brother's for sending Jack to a place he wasn't equipped or prepared to handle just yet. She should've told Ben the signs she had seen but had kept them to herself and she inwardly chastised herself for it.

Her brother walked to the kitchen, shaking his head in disbelief. Then he was back by his sister's side, still standing, still shaking his head. He walked back into the kitchen, paced its length, and came back with an apple in hand. Alexandra urged him to sit down with her eyes, and he obliged, reading her well enough. By her side, Ben took a loud bite from the apple and used his free hand to reach across her and press the ENTER key to pause the game.

"How about idle conversation?" Alexandra asked tentatively. "Would that possibly cull your wrath?"

"Not sure," Ben answered curtly and took another bite, softer this time.

"You must've heard from my conversation with mother that I'm going to be meeting up with Andrea tomorrow. Do you remember her?"

"Sure I do," he said. "Dancer Andrea, right?"

"Yes, that's her."

"I thought you guys might've stopped being friends… given the whole dance thing," he said the last part of the sentence with care, not wanting to bring up the tears their mother had almost made materialize in her eyes.

"It isn't so. She understands my decision, though I didn't explain much. She also didn't ask for much of an explanation. I like that about her. Like that about you, too."

"You abandoned your dream and I focused on my studies so much that I almost lost my friends," Ben said suddenly.

"I was wary to ask you about that," Alexandra said, "I didn't know how much of what I had gathered was true. I remember when I used to call you every other weekend, you talked less and less about going out with friends and more and more about chemical engineering."

"Yeah... I was probably a boring brother on those occasions."

She smiled. "I'm glad you said it, because I wasn't going to."

Ben gave her a small shove playfully on her shoulder. "You're mean," he said.

"I like to call it brutal honesty," Alexandra said.

"I was trying to forget. Making friendships and keeping them was stopping me from forgetting. So, I stopped them. Until my friends called for an intervention. I didn't tell them much about what happened either, but I think telling them the little I did helped in healing more than completely ignoring it did. I don't know. I'm no psychologist. Neither am I the one that's good at reading people. That's you."

"Just because I work at a flower shop that caters to the person's emotions and needs rather than caring for a pricier purchase?"

"Precisely so," he replied, and it sounded like something she would say, which made her laugh.

"You're stealing my style," she said.

"What, interpreting things?" he asked genuinely.

"No, talking eloquently."

"Just because you do it, doesn't mean I can't steal it every now and then." He smiled at her. "When I feel like it." Just as quickly, his smile was gone. "I think about her every night when I try to fall asleep," he said, hopelessness in his voice. He fidgeted in his seat. "At least it feels like every night. Some nights I succeed in falling asleep without her last words haunting me. Other times I have nightmares."

"I used to as well," Alexandra said sympathetically, and she wasn't lying to make him feel better. "My therapist helped with that, and now I only dream and think about her once in a blue moon. Of course, you being here is always a blue moon."

"Sorry," Ben said.

"It's okay!" she said, and put a hand on his arm. "It's not your fault. You're here so I won't ever forget her. I don't want to, I want to see her life as a bright, chipper light, not those last moments. When I see you smile, the night fills with stars."

But her brother looked into the distance, and she wasn't sure he had registered her words. "You've made me smile and laugh more than I have in a long while," he acquiesced. So he *had* been listening, and even turned to look at her before looking into the distance again.

"You even helped me make lunch this time; I'd like to call all of it a great improvement."

"I even let go of her stupid diary," he said, with a sniffle she wasn't prepared for.

"I still haven't let go of the damn rhino," Alexandra added, in frustration that surprised even herself.

"Hey, at least it's a cheery memory. Her diary is full of sadness, disappointment, and despair. I die a little harder inside

157

whenever I skim through it."

"But she wasn't like that. You know that. She only wrote in it when she was a little sadder about life. It was only half-full, wasn't it?"

"I can't seem to recall." Ben leaned down, lifted the shorter table leg, and took out the notebook from where he had wedged it. He thumbed it until he found an empty page and Alexandra was glad to know she had been right. "This one..." Ben said. "I had forgotten all about it."

"What is it?" Alexandra leaned over to read one of the last diary entries. It brought some tears to her eyes. It was *her*, not in the tone that certainly permeated the rest of the diary, but in a good mood. She had written that she had decided to remember the good things, rather than just the bad, like a brother and sister to look out for her, or a teddy bear to keep her company when she felt ignored, or even eating a favorite meal. She ended the entry by saying, "From now on, these are the things I will keep in mind." She had signed it with a flourished signature, a young girl finding herself in her handwriting, in her life in general.

Alexandra finally looked up at Ben, but he was faced the other way. She wondered if he had only skimmed the diary entry. One tear flowed down to her chin. She closed the notebook for him and took it from his lap. Getting up from her seat, she placed the notebook under the rickety leg of the table. She sat back on the wine-colored couch and saw that her brother was looking out into the distance again, eyes a tad red.

***

Once again, I have lost it before I noticed what was going on inside of me. I had been eager to remember, yet these memories brought me nothing but a budding sorrow. I must remember the good times – at the playground, at her studio – rather than the

158

moments that became a turning point for her calloused moods. I cannot stand her fury. Her resoluteness to be cruel for no apparent reason. Her jabs at my sorry frame. I know what she is becoming. What I uncovered of her personality. I don't like it. It wasn't there before. Something within her snapped six years ago and changed her. Something that keeps her from me, for I cannot read her soul any longer. I cannot predict her actions, her reactions, or her attacks. She has become a stranger to me. The only woman I have ever loved is far from my grasp. I must find her again. But this isn't how I will do it. I can't handle this path; it is too much for my fragility.

The kind, female voice urged me to swim back to the sunlight-covered town and so, with some reluctance, I do. I hope to be ready this time. Please forgive my lack of faith.

***

Ben knew it was his fault. He hadn't noticed the signs.

"He showed us he wasn't mentally prepared," Alex told him. "Subtle clues, a lack of new scenery, a hesitance to fill out the memory snippet in that particular book," she taught him. He had noticed these things, but had thought nothing of it.

"I thought he was just growing tired," Ben argued without much heart.

"I hadn't thought of it that way, but it could be that, too!"

"And now we take care and get the memories again?"

"Yes, we do."

Ben sighed in frustration. "Fine," he said. "Go for it." He grabbed his pillow and put it on his lap, worrying his fingers on the fabric.

"I think we should try finding them in order," Alex said,

"then we make dinner. And we resume play tomorrow. How does that sound?"

"Fine, fine." Ben put the computer on his sister's lap. "I can't do it. I'm still upset."

Ben watched his sister as she did both their jobs without complaint. Alex went to the art building and stood at its front steps. The scene of Kat and Jack finding each other after six years appeared on the TV screen, but it played itself out without Jack's narration.

Alex seemed unsure if she should head to the art studio already. "No," she finally said, "she gave him the painting of himself as a kind of apology, right?" she asked Ben.

He shrugged. "I guess," he said. And he wasn't proud of his answer. So, he added, "I think so." He needed to get out of this slump. He needed to remember what she had registered in her diary. Happiness, not sadness, even though for a short time. He must learn to find this happiness and hold onto it with both hands. So, he leaned forward to better focus on the progress his sister was making.

Alex guided Jack to the hillside, where he and Kat had argued about a pamphlet. Again, this memory materialized without narration, only written words and images. A hallway on the right side opened, but this time further down the beginning of the main hallway than it had been the first time it had appeared.

"Huh," Ben said. "There seems to be a missing hallway."

"I realized that," she replied. "Maybe Jack is trying to help us? He certainly knows more than he lets on."

"Perhaps," was all Ben could come up with.

His sister made Jack go to the art studio memory and there, too, an empty space for a memory appeared between *Hillside 1* and *College 2*.

"Huh," Ben said. "Neat."

"Yes, I think we could call it that, and we can say with certainty that each side of the main hallway represents a line of thought, or in this case, memories."

Alex took Jack to the bar, acquired again the memory snippet for its entrance, the book entitled *Bar 1,* without Jack's voice to it. It appeared in a hallway on the left side, taking up the space between the playground memories and the college one, the book entitled *Bar 2.* Ben was very glad for Jack's help, even though he still found the character too sensitive to the players for his taste. Alex paid it no mind and walked to the shining barstool inside the dusty place. She recovered that memory too, but it, *Bar 2,* appeared farther down the left of the corridor than any other memory had reached. Alex acquired the green bottle of beer from the coffee shop.

"Are you ready?" she said. Ben thought she might be talking to him. She was looking in Jack's direction, microphone to her lips. All the same, Ben took the laptop from his sister and placed it on the pillow that was still on his lap. He had forgotten it was there. Jack nodded, slight. "Take a deep breath," Alex was saying. The character did. "Whatever it is, we can get through it together." Jack nodded again, and this time he seemed more confident. "Go to your house," she said. Jack strolled until he reached the street that led to his house. At the corner, he stopped. "Deep breath," Alex reminded him. Jack obeyed. "Go on," she said. He obliged. Walked down the cobblestone street. Ben wondered if he felt like he was going toward his doom. Yet Jack's pace did not waver. Maybe he would go through with it this time after all. He knocked on the door with the beer bottle in hand, just like he said Kat had done.

Jack blinked once, twice, and the scenery did not change or

black out. He blinked a third time. Opened the door. He walked into what Ben assumed was the living room and as he did so, the light that shone through the window ebbed and gave way to night. The room was lit by a light from another room. The memory began.

***

The bottle she had used to knock on my front door at one in the morning was long gone.

We sat across from each other, cross-legged on my living room floor. The bottles between us were empty and my sense of space had begun to leave me. Drinking was not my usual pastime, but it seemed to be for Kat. She worked on another bottle and hardly acted tipsy, though I could tell she was making an effort to remain dignified.

She wore a V-neck, jean shorts, and her usual dark green eyeshadow, though the last was a little smeared. The light coming from the kitchen fell soft on her smooth skin. She was friendlier in the near-darkness than in the harsh daylight.

"College sucks ass," she started. "Whoever invented it deserves a slow death."

"Last semester, Kat," I replied and took a swig, "so get it together."

"Fuck off, Jack," she reprimanded.

I chuckled, which made her giggle. She stopped herself by drinking. I reached for my second bottle, and she handed me the bottle opener.

"This is some good stuff," she exclaimed, holding the bottle at arm's length to inspect it. "I didn't know you had such fine taste."

"My roommate does." I was having a hard time opening my bottle.

"Oh." She took a sip. "Should've guessed you would turn out to be a lightweight."

"That's a word you could use… to describe my situation," I said and just managed to master the bottle opener. If I had taken any longer, I'm sure she would've done it for me. "Is that him snoring?" she asked.

"Name's Carter."

"Thought it was a hibernating bear."

"Carter the Bear." I almost missed the couch as I leaned back onto it.

Kat smiled and it felt like old times. She uncrossed her legs and placed her now empty bottle on the floor. She lay down – knees curled up, head resting on her arms – and looked at me through glass. "He got a girl?"

"Yeah."

"You?"

"Almost had a crush on his at one point."

"Oh?" She lifted her head to look me in the eyes. "Did she turn out to be a slut?"

"Well…" I said and took a sip of my borrowed beer. "Turns out, can't stand her."

"This just gets better," she said and sat back up. She looked at me like a child eager for story time. "Go on."

I sighed. I'm not one to air out my complaints, but she was inviting, and the alcohol made it easier. So, I talked. "She's a daddy's girl raised on caviar. Not caviar, she probably hates the stuff. Non-fat yogurt or something. Damn drama queen that will shriek if a butterfly lands on her. No way to miss her on campus. Walks like she owns the ground her stilettos land on. Name's

Brittany."

"Ah, you mean Brittany the Bitch," Kat nodded.

"Yeah, her," I said. "S'that what they call her?" I was surprised at my own need to gossip like a teen girl. Had to be the alcohol.

"That's what I call her," she murmured. "Keep going." She went for another bottle.

I drank some more of my own and glanced at my watch. It was two-thirty on a weekday. But this was the Kat I hadn't seen in years. Back then, I saw her every week. Now I only saw her walking to and from her classes – she wouldn't acknowledge me when I passed. For some reason, tonight, as she lay awake, she had decided she had nothing better to do but come to my place and look for alcohol.

I stood (with some difficulty) and grabbed a few bags of chips and some water bottles from the kitchen counter before either of us were too inebriated. I handed her two of each and continued. I told her – in speech that was starting to slur and break down – how Brittany was the kind of girl that every man had a crush on; vulnerable, dramatic, enticing, and single. I had finally found the courage to ask her out. She had told me she would think about it and kissed me on the lips, long and hard. That same night I saw her pressed up against Carter outside the bar.

The next day they were a couple. When Carter brought her to our place, it was like we had never met. And whenever Carter wasn't around, I would see her texting. She didn't seem to care that I could see her screen, but she was talking to a number of guys.

"Who?" Kat inevitably asked.

"You wouldn't know 'em."

"So?"

"James, Spencer, Ian..." I said, counting on my fingers, "Gabriel..."

"You kept track."

"Little obsessed. Obsession gone, she's stupid, annoying and needy. That's it. All she is. Don't know why I liked her. She even calls Carter Pookie-Bear," I finished, thoroughly amused.

"Lust is blind," Kat said sagely.

"It is, it is," I replied and raised my empty bottle to her. I didn't recall finishing it. Kat had leaned toward me, over the bottles between us, and had a big grin on, dimple evident.

"You're sexy ranting," she said.

"Am I? Hadn't noticed."

"Yeah," she whispered. "Very fuckable."

I pushed her back by the shoulder gently. She lost her sense of balance and decided that the best option would be to lay down. "You're drunk," I said. "Sleep."

"Nah," she protested.

Before I could say anything else, she closed her eyes.

Chapter 10

Alexandra was glad both boys were working with her again and was a little proud about not resetting the game this time. They had discovered who Brittany and Carter were and this could certainly be called progress. The dust and light had resettled on the house.

"The pamphlet and hillside must've happened right after this," Alexandra said her thoughts aloud. She was right in her assessment: a new hallway appeared in the space before *Hillside 1*. Benjamin dutifully put the words *Jack's House* on the spine of the new red book and saw that the memory was fully written into it.

"Are we going to gloss over the fact that she *did,* in fact, betray Jack's trust?" Ben said to her.

"That I cannot deny," Alexandra replied. "But maybe she thought it to be a good deed?"

"I guess you could call it that," Ben sighed out and from the way he said it, it seemed that he considered it to be anything but.

"You disagree," she said, mentally preparing for a discussion.

"I think we are excusing her actions with some skewed logic," Ben said. "Yes, it's good for someone to know that their significant other is cheating on them, but Carter is still devastated, and I think in part it might be because of how he found out. Kat could've convinced Jack to have a candid conversation with him about it."

"From what we know about her, that might not be something she would do," Alexandra argued. "They're keeping true to the character and besides, I think she did it for Jack's sake, to get some sort of revenge."

"Seems like she did it because she didn't want anyone else hurting the ones they love, which in this case is Brittany hurting her boyfriend. She said as much."

"Perhaps you are getting somewhere," she had to agree. "Maybe she was hurt by someone before and doesn't want it happening to anyone else."

"But she hurt Jack doing so, didn't she?"

"It would appear that her heart is in the right place, but her actions can't seem to reach that righteousness."

"So, you pity her."

"I do, dear brother, and without knowing the complete story, I will continue to do so. Jack said she wasn't always like this, correct? Something happened to her."

"Correct," Ben said. "I guess we'll just have to wait and see," he added. "That aside," he continued, "should we try exploring the house?"

"I hope there is no harm in trying." She told Jack, "Go exploring," and he went into the kitchen first. She looked around with the mouse; everything was dusty and dilapidated, just as expected. There were counters, a single sink, a refrigerator with its door wide open, empty, and a simple stove. With Alexandra prodding him, Jack checked the bathroom; broken sink, empty toilet, wide-open shower; and one of the rooms entirely bare, with outlets on the walls and a built-in closet. He went to the next room and this one showed promise; Jack immediately went for the closet and started opening its drawers in search of something. With the second drawer open, he blinked dust away and transported to the entrance of the room, bringing furniture with the memory; a desk, a bed, a side-table, a full bookshelf. There were objects on the desk and side-table, the bed unmade. Jack read out a new memory.

***

I walked into my room in the place I shared with Carter, my roommate. Something didn't feel right. My door was open, though I remembered having closed it. I turned over the covers on my twin-sized bed. My beige pillow was still there. I looked under my bed. My shoes and the dust around them were where they belonged. I made a mental note to sweep. I looked at my bookshelf. All my textbooks and reading material were organized as neatly as I had left them. I opened my desk drawers. My pencils, pens, erasers, and stray cables were all in their proper places. But one of my notebooks was missing. I found it in my bookshelf. I had missed it the first time because it was thin and had been wedged in there.

"Maybe..." I muttered and opened my closet doors, where I kept my clothes. I noticed what was off straight away. My shirts drawer was ajar. I looked through it, trying to spot each shirt as I rummaged quickly. Instead of my octopus shirt – one of my favorites – there was a handwritten note that said 'You'll see' in torn notebook paper.

I went into the living area to find Carter depressed, laid back on the sofa and watching a soap opera.

"Carter?" I said.

"Yeah?" he mumbled. His stare didn't leave the screen.

"Has anyone been in my room?"

"Yeah, that Kat chick," he said. He looked over at me. "You

know, the one with the green eyeshadow and shit." He looked back at his show.

"You've met her?" I asked, hesitant about the answer.

"Bro, she comes to my parties all the time," he explained like it didn't need explaining.

"Oh." I knew about these parties. I tended to avoid them by locking myself in my room and putting on wireless headphones. I was surprised Kat attended them.

"Yeah..." Carter thought it over, which was a lot of effort for him. "She came in and said you'd asked her to drop something off."

"What was it?"

"Dude, idk. She's your friend, not mine," he said.

"What makes you say that?"

"'Cos she usually stands by your door all quiet and drinking, like she 'spects you to come out, that's why," he said.

Carter stopped talking and I knew I'd get nothing more out of him. I sighed and went back into my room. What are you up to this time? I thought, laying back in my unmade bed.

***

"We acquired that memory rather quickly," Alexandra mentioned, "and it was a short one, too." She glanced at Ben.

"Jackpot?" he asked, hand up for a hi-five.

"Jackpot," she smiled and hit his lifted hand with hers, but she did so hesitantly. "Where has the hallway appeared?"

"Uhm..." Ben said, going into the corridor before the new one, on the right side of the main corridor. "Right after *Hillside 1*," and he went into the hallway that came after, "and before *College 2*. I'm calling this new memory *Jack's House 2*." The game didn't argue with him, and Alexandra smiled her thoughtful smile.

"Kat's apology for the Brittany fiasco and breaking Jack's trust must've been that painting of Jack laughing," Alexandra said happily. "I do think waiting did us some good, for this surely means she is growing up," she said. "Although she didn't need to be so secretive about stealing his favorite shirt."

"Hey, if she wasn't, he would be suspicious," Ben explained.

"Hold on an instant, can I reread the *College 2* memory?" Alexandra inquired, ready to swap her microphone and mouse for the laptop, hands reaching. Ben switched with her, and she took the pillow and computer as if they had always been a combo. "Good," she said after skimming the memory, "she *did* return the T-shirt. I could swear she hadn't." She undid the swap with her brother.

"Maybe you're the one getting tired," Ben said, and he might have been right. The game had started to sap her energy and she felt like she had just finished a day of work, talking to customers and consoling them. She longed to hear one of those elderly gentlemen that sometimes came into Love & Flowers to chat about their life-long, wonderful wife before buying a bouquet for her. Or maybe even a giddy newly-wed who wanted to impress his wife with her favorite flower and had forgotten what it was called, finding it with glee among the many cut flowers available in their shop, and buying chocolate as well.

Jack was a heartbroken customer and Ben was a closed-off one, the kind that came in with a friend who had coerced them to try to mend his relationship. Of course, his problem wasn't a girlfriend, but it was still a girl, and he was clammed up about it, still shut too tightly for her to try and pry open with her bare hands. She would need assistance from powers outside herself and thought about sharing her conundrum with her friend Andrea the next day. She had come to sleep over many times when they were kids, so her friend knew her twin well. Maybe, she hoped, Andrea might be able to help, although she would have to talk about the girl in question, and she didn't feel too keen on doing that. She might be able to circumvent the subject and still get good ideas as to what to do about Ben. It was a thought, one she clung to as she reached over and paused the game, saving it quickly.

"Scrambled eggs on toast for dinner?" Alexandra said, putting the microphone on the keyboard and already getting up. She walked to the kitchen as Ben put away the laptop and, on her way there, she turned off the TV screen manually.

"Don't forget to bring us something to drink this time!" Ben said loudly so she could hear.

"Good gracious," Alexandra said back, stopping at the entrance to the kitchen and turning to look at her brother, crouched by his books, close to the Roman soldier, most likely looking for a book to read among the many he had brought with him. "I didn't even notice I had forgotten," she said.

Ben popped his head up. "That's the problem," he said, gesturing at her with a book.

"What happened to Vonnegut?" she asked, looking to make sure it was still under the table, where he had abandoned it.

Ben stood up, thumbing through the book he had picked: a sci-fi novel he had bought when they were still teenagers. "I'll read more of it when I go to bed," he said. "Well, not bed. Couch." He walked around it to sit down comfortably and read. Alexandra went into the kitchen and started picking out the ingredients for dinner. It wasn't quite time for it yet, but it was the best she could think of doing to get her mind back to rested

171

mode.

***

In no time, Alex had dinner ready. There was a glass of water for each of them on the table. They ate with their plates on their laps. Ben held a piece of toast, laden with eggs, close to his mouth. He took a careful bite, not wanting any eggs to fall off.

"Eating from your lap *cannot* be healthy for your back," he said after chewing. "Why don't you have a dining room table?"

"It would take up the walking space between the couch and the TV. Besides, I don't generally have guests for meals, brother, other than you," Alex replied. She took a bite, some of the egg falling back onto her plate. She didn't seem to mind.

"Not even Mom and Dad?" And he winced as soon as the words were out of his mouth. Touchy subject.

"No worries," she said sagely, for he was worried. "Especially not them," she answered.

"Have you invited them?" he asked, putting his food down.

"To the apartment, or for a meal?"

"Either."

Alex put what was left of her toast down on her plate. "I invited them out to dinner once," she said, "to a fancy restaurant. They canceled on the last minute without much of a real explanation. I've invited them over to my humble abode, but they've always declined, saying they have some important to do or another, so I stopped asking." She picked up a piece of rogue egg and popped it into her mouth. Chewed on it thoughtfully. "Besides," she said, "I have a perfectly good table." She gestured at the low table where she had placed their cups.

"It sure gets the job done," he said with a laugh.

172

She smiled. "What's it like to have graduated?" she asked, changing the subject completely.

"Not much different from being ungraduated," he said. "At least not yet." He pondered this. Things really hadn't felt like they'd changed. He picked up his glass and drank from it. "It's like I'm on break. But I have no return date. Not now or ever."

"And the job hunt?" Alex pried.

"What about it?" he deflected.

"How is it going? Has anything popped up?"

Ben drank some more. "Not really," he said. "There was this one job, but it requires more years of experience than I have. I applied for it anyways, just in case."

She beamed at him. "I'm glad," she said. And he believed her.

"How's work been?" he countered.

"Oh, you know, same old types of customers." She started counting them off on her fingers. "There are the desperate, the downtrodden, the confused, the fatalistic, the deeply in love, and the ones that are about ready for a divorce, unless we can help in any way."

"Sounds like a big responsibility."

"It is, sometimes. Other times we know we can't be of much help and have to watch the customer come to terms with it. Sometimes they even break down in sobs. That's what we have our tissue-box table for – for the weepy."

"Tough luck." He went back to his toast.

"If you want to call it so crudely, yes." She munched on her dinner. They sat in silence for a few moments, eating and drinking.

"How's Andrea?" Ben finally spoke.

"She's engaged to 'the most wonderful man,' as she likes to

put it. I think he's great for her and she's over the moon and most happy with making preparations for the wedding. I think she is going to ask me to be one of her bridesmaids. I am going to have to shop for a turquoise-colored dress or something of the kind. She always liked the strangest of things."

"Maybe that's why you guys got along so well growing up." Ben remembered Andrea as being one of the longest friendships his twin sister ever had. She never judged Alex for her eccentricities because she had her own share.

"Maybe so," Alex said absently, and her gaze became distant. "I hope I do get to be a bridesmaid." Her gaze came back to the present. "It would be an honor."

Ben nodded and ate the last of his eggs on toast.

She put her empty plate on the table and wiped down her skirt. No crumbs fell to the floor. She was perfect like that. He, on the other hand, picked up some pieces of egg and bread from his pants legs. Placed them on his plate, which was still on his lap. Alex picked the plate up for him and skipped to the kitchen with both plates. She was back quick.

"Left them to soak?" Ben chuckled.

"I most certainly did," she replied, shameless.

"How come," he started, then stopped to think of how he was going to say it. "Why aren't you freaked out by Jack?"

Alex sat down on the floor in front of her seat on the couch. She crossed her legs, her back to the table. She looked at Ben. "To answer your question with a question, why are you 'freaked out' by him?"

"It feels like he's a real person, the way he reacts to what we say to him. Especially when he reacts to what we *don't* say to him. Like he's eavesdropping. But only real people eavesdrop. So what is he?"

"A highly sentient computer character?"

"Who has feelings and needs to be taken out of oncoming panic attacks?"

"Precisely."

"That's nuts."

"You could say that."

Ben looked at her quizzically. "I'd even go as far as to call it impossible," he said.

"Not with today's technology," she said, putting up a finger. "Think of Siri. Or Alexa. They don't have panic attacks, but you get my point."

"But ten years ago, when the forum question you found was posted, they didn't have that technology," Ben said, exasperated.

"Maybe it was unfinished. That might be why those players didn't get far. Maybe they remade it now," Alex said thoughtfully. "And they only made one copy each time. For some reason." She looked down at her lap, even more thoughtful.

"And then they dropped it off at a thrift store?"

"I don't know, Ben." Alex sighed. "All I have are theories."

"I'd like to ask him some questions," Ben said decidedly. He had wanted to for quite some time now, to see if it would help them understand all of this better.

"All right," she said. "Why not?" Alex took the laptop and the rest from under the table and gave Ben the mic. She sat on the couch and started the game up again. Ben thought for a second. Then he spoke into the microphone.

"Jack," Ben said.

"Yes?" Jack replied.

"Who is Max?"

Jack looked down at his hands, as if considering the question. "She hasn't told me," he said simply. He put his hands

175

down by his sides and kept on looking down to the dust-covered street.

"Right," Ben said, thinking aloud. "I had too high hopes for that one." Alex chuckled beside him. He pressed on. "What year is it?"

"I... I don't remember." Jack's vision blurred. He shook his head to clear it. "Time here doesn't seem to pass," he concluded.

Ben couldn't decide how he wanted to ask the next question, so he went with his gut. "When was the last time someone played your game?" he asked.

"Played my game?" Jack shook his head slowly. "I... don't understand." So maybe he wasn't so aware after all.

"Um," Ben said, "when was the last time someone helped you recover your memories?" Jack let out a short laugh.

"They never got that far," he said.

"There you go!" Alex said, excited. "The people who first bought the new edition of the game recently didn't get far and put it for sale at the thrift store!" Ben could hear the smile in her voice, but didn't look at her. The next question was important.

He thought hard about it. "Are you... a person?" he asked, then held his breath.

"I'm... I'm me," Jack said.

Ben sighed, unhappy. "That doesn't answer my question. Are you an artificial intelligence?" he asked boldly.

"Please stop with these ridiculous questions," Jack replied and shook his head forcefully. He blinked a few times then went still. "I need to help Kat."

Ben let out another sigh and looked at Alex.

"That wasn't very fruitful," she said.

"No kidding," Ben replied. He put the microphone on the keyboard of her laptop. He quit the game and put everything back

176

under the table.

"Well," Alex said, "here is what I think." She got more comfortable in her seat on the couch. "I generally think of him as one of my customers and I like to read the signs, though it is hard to do when you don't see his facial expressions. But he is very much alive to me, AI or no. When he shakes his head, blinks, hesitates, all of those are signs that I read as danger. We had to learn that quickly after the first abrupt reset, at Kat's house."

Ben sighed. "I guess I'm going to have to go with very well-developed AI. He can't be a real person stuck in a game."

"I agree," Alex said.

"About Kat's house," Ben said, keen. "We never went back to it. Do you think we would be able to help him get through it now?"

"Going back to that house is the last thing I want for Jack," she said. "We still have other clues to follow," she argued, "like the bar."

"Fair enough," he said, putting his hands up in innocence. "I won't talk about it again."

"I am most certainly spent," Alex said with a yawn. She drank the last of her water. "I'm off to continue reading an engaging book in my room. Are you going to do the same?" She got up, her hand on the table as a support.

He grabbed the sci-fi novel from where he had left it on the floor. "Why not?" he said. She smiled at him and strolled to her bedroom, closing the door behind her.

He sighed and opened the book where he had left off. After reading a good amount, taking his now-regular swig of wine, and browsing social media, he went to sleep on the couch.

He awoke with an urge to read her notebook (turned diary). Alex had left a note for him by his small tower of Sweet Tarts. *Gone for brunch with Andrea,* it read. This was fine with him; he didn't want to be caught reading it. He had a hurried bowl of Lucky Charms, a quick shower. Only after he had brushed his teeth did he release the diary from where it held the table still. Ben opened it at a random entry, scrawled with a ten-year-old's handwriting:

I got a D on my math test. I'm scared of showing Mom and Dad. They're gonna be upset.

I showed Alex and she said she wasn't great at math either. This is already the second time I get a bad grade on math this year. They were upset the last time. They will be upset this time, too.

Alex said not to worry because the most they can do is ground me. That's what I don't like. I like watching TV before bed. It makes me calm. I like going to bed when I feel like going to bed. I don't like being sent to my room. Sometimes I need to be around people. I tried explaining this to Alex and Ben. They said they get it, but I don't think they do. Alex can be in her room for hours practicing for a dance recital. Ben can study biology for hours without stopping. I like being in a room with someone to do homework. We're different. I'm different.

Ben silently wondered why he hadn't gone through the process of trying to understand his little sister's needs more. She felt alien in that house, just like he and Alex did. But he had endured and so had his twin. Tricia seemed to need more help. He wondered if having someone of the same age in the house experiencing the same things were what had helped him and Alex to thrive where Tricia had trouble. He shook the thought out of his head and turned to another entry. This one was dated on her eleventh birthday.

It's my birthday today. I invited all eight girls from my class.

We were going to have a cool sleepover, with a movie and popcorn. It's a Saturday. Only two of the girls came. Their parents just picked them up. We had cake and presents, and that's it. Why didn't they want to sleep over? I told them we have some extra mattresses. But they didn't like the idea. Why not? Is it because I'm weird, like Kyle says? I asked him why he picked on me and he said it was because I'm weird. Maybe I am weird. I'm not normal, like they are. I can't even have people agree to sleep over. I thought they were my friends. But they didn't want to sleep over. Maybe I didn't plan enough fun stuff? What do they do for fun? Play with dolls? I don't have any, I threw all of mine away. Maybe play house? I stopped playing that when I was seven. Maybe put on makeup? I don't wear it. Maybe that's why I'm different. Because I don't play with the things they play with. I'm not fun enough.

Ben's heart ached for the little girl. He hadn't known what to do then and he didn't know what he would do now. Perhaps watch the movie she had planned on watching with her friends? He probably wouldn't like it but that was part of sacrifice for the good of another. They had a notion that she might be getting bullied at school, but they weren't entirely sure. They should've done something about it. Would it have helped, in the end? It would likely have made her feel better. It having been an accident, he doubted much would have changed. But he could always hope. Hindsight didn't tend to help. He turned to another page.

Kyle got some other boys in class to pick on me, too; James and Ricky. They kept calling me short and weird and they followed me around the playground. So, I decided to stay inside the classroom and read a book. They kept calling me weird and they wouldn't let me read. They called me a grubby bookworm

179

and said that's why I had no friends. 'Cos I like books more than I like people. I said that wasn't true, that I had friends. They said, "What friends, the ones who went to your party?" Someone told that the girls didn't go to my birthday party. I said that I didn't need those friends, I had my brother and sister. They said, "The weird twins? Aren't they graduating this year? What friends will you have then?" I told him to shut up. I told him to let me read. I just wanted to cry. Ms. Baker came in and asked them what was going on. They ran off to play outside. I put away the book and cried. Ms. Baker asked me what was wrong. I couldn't tell her.

The poor girl didn't have trust in her own teacher. Even worse, she didn't trust her family. They had discovered all these things afterwards when they had found this notebook. They never showed their parents – they would carry the discomfort, him and Alex, alone. The next diary entry he opened was one he didn't want to dwell on. He had forgotten about it.

I wish Mom and Dad let us go into the woods to play. The farthest Ben ever lets me go is to the river, to look for frogs and grasshoppers. I like bugs and animals. I bet I could find some cooler bugs and frogs if I looked in the trees of the woods. Maybe I'll make Ben go with me and we'll climb trees and Alex will draw us playing and maybe we'll find a cool owl or a cool new frog. I wish they would let at least me go to the river by myself but even Ben says I'm too young. I would be very careful. I would even wear the right shoes. The ones Alex makes me wear when we go there. Someday I'll be able to go all by myself, with no help from anyone. Someday I'll climb the tallest tree and pick the coolest leaves. I can take little jars in my backpack and bring home some cool ants or maybe even a spider, to scare Alex. That would be fun.

She had constantly asked them to do the very thing she

talked about on the page. But they wouldn't let her out alone for anything. Maybe, if they hadn't been so strict, disaster wouldn't have struck.

His fingers roamed close to the middle of the notebook, and he found the last entry.

At least Ben and Alex understand me. They're weird like me. Maybe weird isn't that bad. Maybe it just means different. Maybe I'm different. Mom and Dad don't care but if I told Ben and Alex about the boys picking on me in class, I think they would help. I think I'll tell them today when Mom and Dad are gone. Maybe we could finish our homework early and watch a movie. And when they put me in bed, I'll tell them.

Tears welled up in his eyes. He knew the date of this entry all too well; it still haunted him to this day. She had never had time to tell them.

Just then, Ben heard the front door open. Alex was back already. He looked at the clock on the wall: it was close to noon. Since he had eaten a late breakfast, and she had just had brunch, they would probably be diving right into the game. He wiped away the tears before they could fall, before his twin saw them.

Tricia

"Benjamin and Alexandra," their mother said. "You know the rules. Take care of Patricia. No leaving the house. TV until ten o'clock. I want Patricia asleep by then, if not before. Don't wait up for us." The three of them were lined up close to the front door. His mother had her hand on the doorknob. Their father was already outside. "That is all," she said. And she walked out.

Ben looked at eleven-year-old Tricia beside him. All of them knew she didn't like to be called by her full name. Her parents

181

simply didn't care. In turn, the kids didn't know or care as to where the parents were going this time. It was called a 'date,' and that's all they heard of it. At a young age, the twins had learned to be autonomous. They had practically brought Tricia up because of it.

Tricia's lower lip was trembling – either in anger or frustration, he couldn't tell. He thought she might cry, but she was tough. She never did. When she had told their parents about preferring the nickname, they turned her away, saying Patricia was a regal name, one they had picked with care. She said, "That's okay, I don't mind," and smiled a little. But her big brother knew she did mind. Seventeen years of experience had taught the twins not to argue with their parents. Their dad had a temper. Maybe she had learned from them to say she didn't mind.

The three of them let out a communal sigh of relief when they heard the car leaving the driveway. They always dreaded to hear it come back. It was approaching eight o'clock. They had at least two or three hours for themselves.

"Trish, do you have homework left?" Alex asked.

"Some," Tricia said. "But it's math."

"Oh," Alex replied. They all knew she hated math – with a passion. "Maybe Ben can help you with it," Alex said and headed for her room.

"Could I hang out with you for a little bit?" Tricia asked before she lost Alex.

Alex looked at the grandfather clock. "Yeah, sure!" she said. "You can sit on the beanbag. I have homework too but maybe you could help *me* out."

Tricia giggled and she was a little girl again. Alex probably knew that's what they all needed. The little girl certainly did.

"Hey!" he said, "I was gonna ask her to help with my SAT

Prep." He sat down on the hard sofa. "Now I don't know what to do."

"Do it yourself," said Alex. "She's coming with me." Alex strode to her room.

"Yeah, bozo," said Tricia, "I'm too young for SAT." She hurried after Alex with a spring in her step.

Ben went to his room and put his headphones on. He needed music to focus on his work. Ben and Alex were juniors in high school and the school year was ending. He'd done the SAT before, but he wanted to do better this time. Alex had decided to be a dance teacher assistant right out of school. Their parents were rich and had good connections, so the job was already lined up. He wished he had her to do the SAT Prep with. It was only getting harder.

He lost himself in his textbook. Sometime later (he couldn't tell how long), Tricia pushed his door open and peeked in. Ben pulled his headphones down to his neck. "What happened?" he asked her.

Tricia walked in and sat on Ben's unmade bed. She grabbed his pillow and pressed it against her chest. "Stupid Brenden called," she said. Brenden was Alex's boyfriend. "I got sick of all the mushiness." She looked down at her purple, sparkly shoes. "I don't like him."

Ben put his pencil and book down. "Have you told her that?"

Tricia nodded.

"Then the grave is hers to dig. I don't think he's a good guy, either."

Tricia was silent and started fidgeting with her hair. She only did so when she was restless or anxious.

"Bring your homework in here," Ben said. "You don't mind the mess, do you?"

Tricia put the pillow down. "No, I don't," she said. "My room is worse."

"Then it's set," Ben said with a flair. "Come do your math here. I'm very busy but we can at least talk if you'd like." He reached into his backpack and pulled out his earphones. "I'll even put these on for you."

"One earphone out?" Tricia asked.

"Yup," said Ben.

Tricia walked out of Ben's room, happier. She came back with her book and notebook. "Can I have one of your pencils?" she said. "I... lost mine. At school." Recently she had a tendency of losing things at school. She was small for her age. He wondered if she was being bullied and wasn't telling them. He would ask her about it when she finished her homework. For now, Ben handed her a sharpened pencil. Tricia sat on his bed. She took his Sweet Tarts box from his desk and started working.

Over his music, he could hear her scribble away. Sometimes she would stop, probably to think. Her math teacher usually gave them a lot to do. So, he was surprised when Tricia got up abruptly.

"Finished?" Ben asked. He took out the second earbud he hadn't remembered putting in.

"Yeah," she said. "I'm gonna watch TV."

Ben looked at his watch. "You got an hour." He sighed. "Parental orders." Tricia left with a nod. They never knew when their parents would come back. It was safer to obey the few rules they had set. Tricia didn't like being up when they came back anyways. Soon enough, he heard the TV. He put his second earbud back in.

An hour later, Ben was satisfied with his studying. He pulled his earphones out and went to search for Tricia. The TV was off, but he hadn't noticed its silence. He went to his little sister's door. It was decorated with flowers and bees. Ben knocked lightly but heard no answer. He didn't want to wake her. So, he walked to Alex's room and knocked.

"Come in," she said.

"Hey, Alex."

"Hm?" Alex replied. She was sitting cross-legged in the middle of her room with a copy of *Lord of the Flies*. He had forgotten all about the reading they had for tomorrow.

"Did Trish say good night to you?" he asked her.

"Not exactly," she said. She looked up from her book. "She asked if she could sleep on my beanbag tonight and I had to decline because I still have too much to do. Dad would be angry if she were still up because of me." She paused. "Why?"

"Well," he said, "she did math in my room, and I don't think she finished. Then she went to watch TV. But she didn't come back to my room." She usually gave him a kiss good night, without fail. "I knocked on her door and got no answer."

"The TV went off about forty-five minutes ago," Alex said, getting up. "I've been reading ahead so I haven't been out of my room. Maybe she is just too tired?" Alex could only study in her room because she said the rest of the house felt too alien. He didn't blame her.

None of his little sister's behavior sat well with Ben. "She didn't come in to say good night?" he asked again.

"No…" said Alex. "She tends to, doesn't she? Even when she knows we're busy with homework." Alex deliberately placed her book on a shelf. She looked pensive.

They both went back to their little sister's door and knocked. No answer. They looked in.

The bathroom door was ajar. By its light, they saw a jumble

of covers on her bed. Her favorite stuffed animal, Scottie the Rhino, wasn't there. The room was a mess, per usual, but it looked messier tonight. There were clothes strewn everywhere. Her backpack wasn't in its usual place by her door. He didn't see Tricia's head peeking out of the covers.

"Trish?" Alex said, loudly. No answer. She turned the main light on.

"Tricia!" Ben shouted.

But she wasn't there.

***

Brunch with Andrea had been fruitful, as Alexandra had anticipated. They talked about her friend's upcoming wedding and, as she had predicted, she was invited to be a bridesmaid, to which she gladly said yes. Thankfully, she wasn't invited to be maid of honor – that position was left to the bride's sister – for she was a terrible planner.

Then they talked about Alexandra's work, which made it easy for her to segue to Ben. She told Andrea she knew he needed her help but that she didn't know what to do. She finally told another person in her life about what happened to her little sister, a little more than five years ago. Her friend had listened intently, without interrupting, only nodding here and there, urging her silently to continue her story. Andrea's eyes were glistening with tears by the time Alexandra had finished and her friend wiped her eyes dry with a steady hand. Alexandra felt a stinging in her own eyes, but she didn't bother addressing it.

"I think," Andrea said between sips of tea, "that Ben might be feeling doubt, sorrow, but most importantly, guilt. At least a little of each," she added, for Alexandra was looking at her in astonishment.

"Whyever would he feel guilty, even if just a smidge? It was an accident and therefore no one can be to blame." She had lost interest in her scone and left it, half-eaten, on the table they shared at the teashop. She really was bad at understanding people, at least those close to her.

Decidedly, she said, "If he isn't aware of that, I will have to make him notice. But," she said, twirling the spoon in her tea, thinking, "I don't want to be the type of person who pries and tries to rip off a bandage on a wound that isn't ready."

"I know you. You're probably very impatient to do so and will grow even more impatient as time passes," Andrea said with a knowing smile. She was right.

Alexandra leaned back on her chair and crossed her arms defensively, with an undignified pout. "I will have to endure in silence," she said. "I'm sure he will open up eventually," she said with hope in her voice, enough to make her uncross her arms. "I will wait. He's already started opening up, due to this game we're playing."

"A game is making him open up?" Andrea asked, puzzled.

Alexandra told her about *Comatose* and how it had led him to share about his breakup. "I don't know how, but I feel like this game is going to continue to help with that later on, though for now that is just a feeling of blind hope and desire." She huffed in frustration and finally picked up her meal again.

"We can hope," Andrea said, placing a hand on her friend's. They finished their cream and jam scones, drank the last of their tea, and paid. Then they both went their separate ways, Andrea to her wedding planning and Alexandra to her brother and *Comatose*.

Ben was quickly tucking the notebook back under the table's short leg when she walked around the books that lined the floor and its ludicrous bookend to sit down. He didn't mention the notebook so neither did she, and her impatience grew, just as Andrea had predicted. She smiled at the thought and said, "Say hello to bridesmaid Alexandra."

"Congratulations," he said, and tipped an invisible hat toward her.

"Thank you," she said with a mock bow, awkward from her sitting position. "Did you remember to eat?" she asked him. As a reply, he pointed to the dirty bowl in front of him, still on the table. She would have to teach him to put his dishes away after use. "Have you unlearned everything about dirty dishware that Mom and Dad taught you?"

"Sorry, sorry, got distracted," he replied, reaching to grab the bowl, but he stopped. "I can put it away now *or* we could play some *Comatose.*"

"Why can't I have both?"

"Message received," Ben said and took the bowl to the kitchen.

Alexandra took the computer from where she had tucked it away under the small table, put her brother's fluffy pillow under it, and had it ready to put on his lap when he returned.

"Jumping right to it, okay, okay," he said, receiving the pillow and laptop combo, and she kept the microphone and mouse.

"Good afternoon, Jack," she said into the mic cheerfully.

"Every hour here feels like noon," Jack told them with a tired voice. "But I am always glad to hear your voice," he continued, to their surprise.

"Thank you," Alexandra replied, uncertain.

"Did that just happen?" Ben asked.

"Yes, it did. Carry on."

Her brother obliged, heterochromatic eyes still wide in disbelief. "I say we try finding the *Bar 1* which fits..." he paused to think, "right between the playground memories and the college one."

"Right you are," she said. "Jack?"

"Yes."

"What say you about finding a fake ID card in the mess that is the café?" she asked him, earnestly.

"I can try," he said and was already walking from his house – where they had saved the game last – to *Tom's Café*. He was in it in no time, crouching under a table to browse through and overturn some books, a wallet, a basketball, a broken chain, and a plastic daisy.

"That table over there was never searched properly," Ben said, pointing.

"Which one?" Jack asked him.

"The one closest to the far wall," Ben said, without the usual surprise in his voice. Maybe he was getting used to it by now. Jack found the ID card under a framed picture of a puppy, on the table Ben had suggested. The screen flashed to black, and the words appeared and read: *All I managed was to keep my head up and pretend like I owned the place*. In another blink, the screen turned back to the dirty café.

"Jackpot!" Ben exclaimed and Jack nodded, once, as if agreeing with him. "Please stop doing that," Ben said just loud enough for Alexandra to hear. She let out a laugh. "And you, stop doing *that*," he told her.

"Yes sir," she said, although she had a hard time stopping. Ben was certainly ignoring her the best he could as he put the memory snippet into the *Bar 1* book. When she finally managed to compose herself, Alexandra told Jack to go to the bar. His gait was steady and determined and Alexandra couldn't help but think that they were on the right track. Fake ID in hand, Jack stood at the entrance to the bar and the screen blinked into night, Kat by his side.

***

"It won't work," I told Kat. "They card you as soon as you walk in."

"You don't know that," she hissed. She was wearing a knee-length dress, dark blue, to look older. She wore a pair of her mother's high heels, and I was surprised she could walk in them as easily as if she wore sneakers. She had put on green eyeshadow and a dab of lipstick. I wore a white button-down shirt and dark blue jeans. These were the only clean, dressier clothes I could find. "Live a little," she whispered to me as we came closer. She held my hand to add to the charade. I hardly blushed and was amazed at how comfortable I felt around a girl I met only three months ago.

I looked at the fake ID she had made me and was impressed at her seamless handiwork. Maybe someone with a trained eye might be able to tell it was off. But I was sure we wouldn't even have a chance to use it. We weren't older than sixteen.

As I approached the open door to the bar, I noticed there was no one guarding it. Maybe I was erroneous in my thinking about how all bars worked. Maybe the bouncer was on his day off. Maybe we had a chance after all.

We walked in, Kat with that confident and leisurely stride of hers. All I managed was to keep my head up and pretend like I owned the place. I was hardly fooling myself. The lighting inside was dim. The place had barely opened for the night so there were only a few there other than us. The next thing I noticed was the strong scent of alcoholic beverages, some stale, others swift and sweet. While I was trying to take it all in, Kat was already on a high barstool in front of the bartender. I hurried to her side.

"Hey, Jimmy," she was saying. In a second, I noticed she didn't know him – he was wearing a nametag. "Can I get a shot of vodka?" The man didn't look at her. He prepared the man beside her his beer and gave it to him. "What ya say?" she prodded.

Jimmy finally looked at her. His facial expression said it all. "ID," he demanded.

"Aw, come on, man," she objected but handed hers over. He glanced at it once and gave it back.

"You're kidding, right?" Jimmy chuckled and got a towel. He started cleaning a glass. "Get out of here and go back to your high school reading." Kat looked aghast. "Come back in, like, five years, huh?" he waved her off.

I started to snicker. Then I couldn't hold it in and laughed. I laughed all the way to the playground, where Kat immediately went for the swings.

Chapter 11

Ben was laughing too, though softly. Alex looked at him and grinned.

"Let the poor girl be!" she told him. "Wait a minute, Benjamin, what is going on?" His sister was looking at the laptop screen. The *Bar 1* book was back on its bookshelf and the *Kat* book had appeared, spine toward them. It opened itself up and turned around to show them a hurried writing of this new memory into its pages, right after the first two playground memories that were already there. It stopped on the last sentence and waited, open, fountain pen gone. Ben pressed ENTER and the book went back into its usual place on the menu screen. He pressed the key again and he was looking at the faded spines next to the only red book.

"Shall we place the next memories in?" Alex asked, unsure. Ben tried going into the next hallway and picking up the red book entitled *College 1*, which talked about Kat's return after being absent for six years. As soon as it opened, the *Kat* book reappeared and it stored this memory away, too. He went farther down the hallway, to where the *Bar 2* book was. After it, there was some empty main corridor, which must mean they were still missing memories.

Nothing happened when he picked the *Bar 2* book up.

"Maybe the ones on the right of the main hallway are next?" Ben asked. He was already going to the beginning of that side of the corridor. He entered the first hallway to find *Jack's House 1* memory, where Jack had inadvertently told Kat about Brittany cheating. The *Kat* book wrote this memory in. Ben was smiling as he went to the next hallway on the right and the *Hillside 1* memory, with Jack confronting Kat, was soon in the *Kat* book, too. Next was the *Jack's House 2* memory, with Jack finding Kat's note. Then came *College 2*, with Kat apologizing by giving Jack a painting.

He tried the *Bar 2* memory once more and now it fitted itself into the *Kat* book easily.

The main corridor loomed ahead of him, with empty space for new hallways beyond.

"We still have more story to fill out," Ben told Alex. Of course she must've guessed it too, but he felt the need to share his thoughts. He hadn't done much of that in a long time.

"You are correct," she said, "for we do not yet know why Kat left and came back."

"Right." He chewed at the inside of his cheek, thinking about what he was going to say next. "I think we should go to Kat's house."

Alex, as he predicted, wasn't on board immediately. "We seem to have a small number of options left, and that is indeed one of them."

"What are the other options?" Ben asked, genuinely lost.

"I think the playground has one more memory in store for us." Jack must've heard, for he shook his head vigorously.

"Jack, it's okay," Alex said into the microphone. "So not that one yet," she said with a sigh.

"No," Jack replied.

"Kat's house it is, then!" Ben said, cheerful for having succeeded. The surprise at Jack's interaction with them was slowly wearing off.

His sister was getting Jack ready. "Take deep breaths. That's it, relax your body. No need to hurry. Let's stroll to Kat's."

Jack's progress was slow, but he arrived at the front door of the house. He blinked once and Kat appeared; the world turned dark. The girl and the brick of the house were illuminated by the streetlamp. Words appeared on the screen and Kat's voice rung out, *Are you sure it wasn't normal flirting?*

Jack blinked the screen back to Solstice; his breathing was hurried as he continued blinking.

"Calm down," Alex was saying. "Steady your breathing. That's it. You made it. It's all right."

"Where are the white roses?" Jack asked them when he had steadied himself. He was looking at his hands. "I could feel them with me."

"I think I saw some white roses at the café," Alex said. "Let's go find them," she told Jack. Once at *Tom's Café*, she helped him out by moving his gaze with the mouse. While they searched, Ben put the snippet into the book he had entitled *Kat's House,* in a new hallway that had emerged a little ways away from the *Bar 2* hallway.

"We're missing a memory between the bar and this new one."

"It certainly will tell us why Jack was confused between Kat's normal flirting and something more," Alex concluded.

Jack finally found the roses and he held them firmly in his hand. *She took the roses and slammed the door shut,* appeared on the screen in the dusty coffee shop. Jack read it out and then the words vanished.

Ben put *took the roses* into the book and the narrated sentence emerged on the page. "Now is time for the moment of truth," Ben said, looking at the TV screen. Jack was completely still. Alex had to coax him to move.

"Go back to Kat's house. You've got the roses now, so you must surely be ready."

"I am," Jack said. Was he reassuring them or himself? He made his way to the house, but not before stopping at the hillside for a split second. Ben hardly noticed it happen before Jack was on the move again.

"Did he—" he started to say.

"Yes, he did," his sister answered the unfinished question. She made Jack look over his shoulder to the hillside. His gaze lingered before Jack turned his head back around, facing forward. He kept walking and reached Kat's house. This time, he knocked on the door before blinking to the night scene. He was looking at Kat in a pair of sweats.

***

Her eyes were dazzling from the streetlamp, and I swear they were tinted red.

"What do you want?" she huffed. She rested her side against the doorjamb and looked down on me over her slender nose. I felt drink emanating from her, but mostly hostility. I kept my gaze locked on her deep brown eyes.

"Well." I avoided her glare to take a closer look at what she wore – sweats. "I'm here to pick you up." She still managed to look elegant, her body poised in slight indignation. "No need to change," I continued, "I didn't plan on anywhere fancy."

She closed her eyes and I noticed she didn't have her usual green eyeshadow on. She sighed. "What the fuck are you talking about?" she whispered, vicious.

"I'm taking you out." I indicated my button-down. "We agreed last night," I added.

She walked a step back into her house, a hand on the doorknob, her now slackened frame silhouetted in dim lighting. She seemed to be blushing. "I always flirt with you when I'm tipsy," she said.

"I know." I extended the hand that was hidden behind my back in her direction. I wasn't going to lose her. "But this time you asked me out," I said, nervous. "I said yes. I hoped being sober wouldn't change your mind."

"Are you sure it wasn't normal flirting?" she asked with a tentative smirk. I looked at her, concerned.

"Yeah," I replied. Her hand was still on the doorknob, but she was studying the white roses I offered.

"Let me find a glass for those." She took the roses and slammed the door shut. Kat disappeared inside.

I almost exhaled in triumph, but I could tell there was something amiss. She seemed like a completely different person than she was the night before. I stood outside her door for about fifteen minutes, hoping she had found a glass for the roses and was taking her time changing out of her lazy clothes and into going-on-a-casual-date-with-Jack clothes. I stood there until it started to drizzle. She didn't come back out.

***

Jack blinked the screen back to brightness and heat. "Ouch," Ben said.

"Indeed," Alex replied.

"I told you he was being rejected."

"You were right, dear brother, and I'm not glad you were."

"Neither am I," he had to agree. "Hillside time?"

"Hillside time."

***

Jack started moving away from the house, back to the hillside, before Alexandra told him to. She waited for him to reach it with weary steps and when he arrived at the barren hill, he sighed as he made to sit down. As his hand made contact with the sand on the ground, grass emerged, and the world went dark again. Jack narrated as the words faded onto the screen, *Her gaze was locked on the wire fence below and what lay beyond it: the playground.*

"Do you remember seeing part of a wire fence?" Ben asked her, determination in his voice, and she had to smile. "'Cos I do," he added and this time she looked at him, locked her eyes with his mismatched ones.

"Lead the way, Sir Benjamin," she said, handing him the microphone and mouse, exchanging them for the laptop and pillow. She plugged the computer in before it decided to die mid-game, and found the newest hallway where the empty space between *Bar 2* and *Kat's House* had been. "We have found your missing memory," she told her brother. She hovered up to the only red book on the bookshelf and wrote in *wire fence and what lay beyond.* The sentence corrected itself and filled out until it was whole.

"That's settled," Ben said, "now to Tom's Café." She hadn't noticed he had waited for her to type in the memory before moving and her spirits rose a little. He had been thinking about her and wanted her to keep up with what he did, which made him more thoughtful than herself. She usually ran around while he did his part of the game and now she chastised herself for doing so, for he was playing, too. He deserved to know what was going on with her end, just as much as she wanted to be apprised about what happened on his. She made a mental note to wait for him next time.

"Enter through the hole in the wall," Ben was saying – an odd thing to say, but soon Alexandra understood why. Inside the café, her brother made Jack look down at the floor beside the hole and there was the piece of wire fence.

"That is a very good memory," she uttered and saw Ben grin a little in response.

"Thanks," he said. Jack touched the piece of fence and read out the words on the screen as the café disappeared and brought the grassy hillside into view, '*Here's to growing old,*' *I said, and clinked my bottle against hers.* The café came back, muffling out the darkness of the comforting night and drink.

Then, Jack was already making his way out through the hole and Ben leaned back on the sofa, letting the character do all the work. "I didn't know being on the right track was so gratifying," Ben said.

"It most certainly is," she said, putting in the new snippet of memory, "and it's quite nice to see him go to the next stop so readily. I bet that if we could look at his face, we would see some smug determination in his eyes. It feels like a joyous improvement from how he was in the beginning, unsure and afraid. And oddly enough, it feels like we're helping."

"We are," Ben replied. "He's getting his memories back."

"My question for you is if he *wants* them back and if he's happy to have them return."

As a reply, Jack threw the piece of wire fencing down the sandy hill. It stopped mid-air at the bottom and the rest of the wire fence reconstructed around it. Darkness overtook the fence and spilled out onto the rest of the TV screen, bringing grass and Kat with it.

***

Kat had been drinking before I arrived, but at least this time she had asked me to join her. She had a big bottle of whiskey with her and a couple of beers for me.

"Heya," she said and patted the grass beside her. She was wearing a loose T-shirt, a pair of dark blue jeans, and her green flats. Her gaze was locked on the wire fence below and what lay beyond it: the playground.

"Done with classes for the day?" I asked.

"Pretty much," she replied. She was rubbing a piece of grass in between the thumb and index finger of her free hand. With the other she took swigs of whiskey. I twisted off the top of my beer and took a big gulp. With all the recreational drinking me and Kat did, I had gotten an affinity to drink, and it didn't make me want to gag anymore. "You?" she inquired.

"Yup," I said. I hadn't finished classes, but I was getting a bout of senioritis. I had the skips to back it up.

"I miss coffee," Kat said. She didn't have to say much else because I knew what she meant. She missed being a teenager with little to worry about but joining up with a friend once a week in growing darkness to chat and gossip and be morose. We thought ourselves invincible back then.

"Here's to growing old," I said, and clinked my bottle against hers. I could see her smile and dimple from my peripheral vision.

"We aren't old just yet," she murmured. "We're getting there, though," she said. "Swiftly and surely, yes we are."

Nowadays there was the wire fence keeping the kids away from this hill and it didn't feel right. Years ago, we had arrived right before dusk started to set in and climbed up this hill from the playground. From up here you could see the sun set red and golden. But we had our backs to it now and saw its effects on the playing equipment below. The shadows to the swings elongated. The treehouse started to look dark and ominous. The last family there left the sandbox, got into their car, and drove away.

"Pussies," she said. "It's just darkness."

I laughed. Kat smirked. The years had changed her. She smiled and talked less and usually only after she had a drink. She hardly laughed anymore. But I couldn't tell what it was that changed her. She never told me. I never asked. It wouldn't have been polite. I was waiting for her to find the courage to speak up about it, but feared she wouldn't.

Her whiskey bottle was half gone. She should be acting tipsy by now, but I could tell she was keeping composure. She took another swig, like the seasoned drinker she was. "I've got a proposition," she said, and she slurred the last word out. "How about..." she stopped mid-sentence.

"Mhm?" I questioned.

"How about... how 'bout we go out. On a date." She giggled. "Me and little Jackie on a date just by our lonesome."

I laughed. "You serious?" I said when she didn't revoke what she had just proposed.

"Why not?" Kat said. "Like old times. Coffee. Playground. Date."

"I wouldn't call those dates."

"Yaknow they were."

"No, they weren't."

"What were they?" she interjected and stared at me with

those dark eyes, a challenge.

"They were..." I started.

"Uh-huh..."

That stare egged me on. "They were hangouts. With a friend."

"A friend that bought you lattes?" She took a drink from her bottle.

"Yeah," I said, and tried to hide my blushing by taking a sip from my beer.

"Come on, dummy, you're in denial," she said. "You know anyone would kill to go on a date with me."

"Why's that?" I asked and took a swig.

"'Cos I'm mysterious."

"And? Loads of people are."

"And I'm cute."

"Not arguing with that one."

"I have good fashion taste."

"Guys don't care about fashion."

"My eyes can read into your soul," she concluded. She threw her head back.

"I wouldn't doubt they did."

"Is that a yes?"

"Why not?" I said and smiled at her. She grinned back and drank some more.

***

"That's why the poor boy was confused!" Ben was saying in exasperation, putting down the microphone, letting go of the wireless mouse. The *Kat* book emerged on the computer screen, and it wrote this memory in as neatly as it had written all the others, unaware of the tragedy it brought to the person the memory belonged to. "She flirts regularly by asking him to cuddle, to sleep over, even calls him 'fuckable' – sorry for the language, but she used it first – and then she asks him out on a proper date, and he says yes, and then she acts like nothing happened? No wonder they're not together."

Alexandra put a hand on her brother's arm. "Relax," she told him, "it's just a game. Besides, she might... not want to remember? Maybe because of that something that happened to her that we know nothing about. Look, I don't know. And before you look at me like that, yes, I am aware that I am defending her yet again."

Ben shook his head. "Still waiting for that explanation?"

"I think all three of us are," she said, crossing her arms.

"I have a feeling Jack knows but isn't telling us," Ben said, looking at the TV screen accusingly.

"Then let us make him tell us," Alexandra said, cheerfully; she had already placed the *Kat's House* memory in the *Kat* book. "It is time. For the playground." Jack must've heard her, for he started walking, slowly, wary.

***

Kat isn't Kat any longer. She has changed. I want to find out why. The male voice has no pity for her, but the female one does, and I will listen to her guidance once more. With her help, I will get to the bottom of this. I am ready to go back to the playground, where it all started and where I hope it won't end. I have a bad feeling about this, like this is all that's left, that I am about to lose her completely. I'm hoping against hope that it will not be so.

***

In what seemed like a longer while than it surely was, Jack finally reached the playground, but he did not enter, standing outside it. He momentarily put his hands over his eyes, shook his head, blinked, and the skies darkened. Night overtook the screen and there was Kat, waiting.

***

She wasn't inside the playground on the grass like I had assumed she would be. I met her outside it; she was sitting, her back against the wooden fence. Her text hadn't given me much about what had happened or what she wanted, so I had come seeking answers. When I reached her, I tried not to glare. The green eyeshadow was back. Her curly hair was in a bun on top of her head. It made her look vulnerable. She wore a maroon, long-sleeved shirt that covered her hands against the chill of the night, and grey sweats. Her feet were bare, toes tapping the sidewalk, uneasy. She had on a shy smile.

She was waiting for forgiveness. I had none to give her.

"Please sit," she implored. Her dark eyes were sad. It looked like she had been crying. I acquiesced, sat down. "Jack," came that same tone of voice.

"Yeah?" I said, not looking at her. She put a hand on my arm, and I flinched back from it.

"I know I don't deserve it," she said.

"You're damn right," I retorted.

"But please listen."

I listened while her voice was strong, and I kept on listening when it went limp and distressed. She wiped a few tears on her shirtsleeves. I put an arm, tentatively, around her. She told me why she had left six years ago and why she was going to leave again now. In between sniffles, she told me about her little brother Max.

"Max was my sweet pea," she said. "He loved me, and I loved him, like any big sister would. He was just four. I used to take him to the playground after school, so I could push him on the swings and have him get some energy out by going in and out of that treehouse. You know the one." She glanced back at it quickly and then shuddered. She continued, looking down at her hands on her lap. "He would always light up when I came back from school to take him to the park. Sometimes I would sneak out of school just so I could be with him. And other times, I was the one to put him to bed, when Mom worked a night shift. I'd watch TV with him until he'd fall asleep." She smiled a little and the reminiscence seemed to be doing her some good. I didn't interrupt.

"His giggles were my greatest joy. I remember once, when he laughed so hard at something I did – I don't even remember what it was. Milk came out his nose. He stopped laughing and gripped his nose, about to cry, but when I started laughing at what happened, he broke into giggles and forgot all about his stinging nose. Until we stopped laughing and he started crying a little. I tickled him until he agreed that the stinging was just his nose's way of saying it was laughing, too. So stupid. But it worked." Then her face went somber. "I don't know why I'm telling you all this. I never told anyone that before."

"Keep going," I urged her.

"Sometimes…" She looked like she was going to cry. But she collected herself. "Sometimes I would get out of the house at night when Max was already asleep and Dad was in one of his

drinking binges, with the TV at the highest volume, not caring about anyone else in the house, like me, trying to do some last-minute homework. I don't know how Max slept through it, but he did. Mom had given up arguing with dad about it. I told you he was a mean drunk, right?" She looked up to me and I nodded. "Well, he was drinking that night, too, and I tried telling him to lower the volume on the TV, but he threatened to put it louder. He was harmless, really. Well, I thought he was. That's why I left the house that night for a walk like always, to clear my head. Mom was working the night, but Max was safe, right? He never woke up before.

"I was selfish, I know that now, I should've stayed with Max. If I had been there..." She bit her lower lip to stop the tears from coming. I wanted to tell her she could cry but she probably wouldn't have listened. "If I had been there, it might've been different.

"I knew something had happened the moment I came into the house. He was at the bottom of the steps, and he wasn't moving. I hardly heard the TV blaring; my thoughts were trying to make sense of what I was seeing. I must've closed the door. I know I ran to him when my thoughts finally settled on the worst possible explanation. I could see that his little neck was broken... his head was at a wrong angle." She shuddered at the memory, and I tightened my arm around her. "I know I screamed, 'cos Dad told me to shut up. That brought me back to my senses. I started trying to piece it together, though my thoughts were an anguished blur. He had woken. He had fallen down the steps. Dad hadn't heard because he was drunk and watching TV.

"I didn't know if I should cradle the body and cry – I couldn't accept that it was just a body... or if I should yell at Dad for not being there for him. But how could I judge him? I hadn't been

205

there either. I walked closer to Max, shivering all over. I knelt by his lifeless body. And I finally realized that this was real. He was gone. He was a body now." Her gaze was on her feet, and she hugged herself, hunching over. I put the arm that had been holding her by my side.

"Can you believe what that bastard did when he heard me wailing, on the floor with his baby boy's head on my leg? He got up and told me to shut up, that he was watching TV. Then he saw Max, 'cos he said, 'That little prick had it coming.' Only then did I grow suspicious. My new thoughts stopped me crying. I asked Dad if he had anything to do with this. He stood there, staring into nothingness. He looked me dead in the eyes and said that the little prick had been calling for Mommy at the top of the stairs and that he had gone up and given him a good shake to teach him a lesson. I remember his words clearly, as if it were yesterday: 'I let go. He fell down. At least he stopped whining, the little prick.' Anger overtook my grief. I gently placed Max's head back on the ground and faced my father. I told him he was a 'bloody bastard,' that he had murdered his son and hadn't even blinked. He huffed at me and sat back down on his Lay-Z Boy.

"I knelt on the floor beside Max and called my mom on the phone. Tears starting coursing down my cheeks as I told her what happened. She tried telling me to calm down and speak slowly, but I was beyond consoling. I managed to tell her to 'just come back home.' That did it, because as I sat with the upper half of Max's body on my lap, with no tears left, she came home. She let out a cry when she saw him. I told her that the bastard was responsible. Instead of confronting him, she knelt down beside me and told me to pack my bags. Her voice was faltering, and I had a feeling she was keeping composed for my sake. She put a shaky hand on Max's head, then hurried upstairs.

"We left town that same night. We laid his body in the backseat, a seat belt over his waist to keep him still. Neither of us said a word on the ride to my grandmother's, a state over. At that point, I was numb. Mother finally let herself cry when she got out of the car and threw her arms around grandma. She had called to say we were coming over, but gave no details. The sun was dawning over the horizon, and I hated it for doing so; my world had just shifted to eternal night. After I explained what happened to both her and Grandma, my grandma did the sensible thing and asked if Mom was going to press charges. Mom shook her head vigorously. She was more afraid of him than I had noticed. I, for one, was happy the bastard was out of our lives for good. The next day, we buried little Max in the plot next to my grandfather."

Kat finally looked at me and I could see tears threatening to fall down her cheeks. Her lower lip quivered. I sat there, not knowing what to say. She took a deep breath to steady herself. *"That's why I left,"* she said.

"But you came back," I said, tentative.

"My psychologist told me I should try closing that chapter in my life. My father had already died of liver failure, of course. It was the perfect timing. But, Jack, I wasn't ready." A tear fell down her cheek. *"I couldn't live in that house without having to drink the memories of my dead brother away. I thought I could handle it. I told my therapist I could handle it. But I couldn't. I didn't even last half a year. It was six years ago, and I couldn't handle it."*

"You do know no one is wanting you to," I told her.

"What?" she asked, brushing a tear away.

"No one is expecting you to be able to handle it."

"I am," she replied, voice weak.

"Don't. Grief takes time to leave."

"You're starting to sound like my therapist," she smiled a small smile, dimple showing for a brief second.

"You know you called his name in your sleep?" I asked, unsure if I should bring it up but doing it all the same.

"Oh gosh. I can't even escape while I'm unconscious," she said, anguished.

"That's okay," I said, in a hurry to repair what I had done. "That means your brain is healing."

She wrung her hands. "I hope you're right," she said. Then she stood. "I'm leaving tomorrow," she said. I wished I had the courage to tell her to stay. "But I wanted to tell you... what happened first. I feel like you deserved it after the shit I put you through."

"Want to grab a latte?" I asked, hopeful.

"Why not? Live a little, eh?"

I chuckled. The smile that came to her face was one I could lose myself in. I blinked and it went away. I stood and offered her a hand. She took it and we walked to Tom's Café.

***

Both screens went blank. *Thanks for playing* appeared on them, and the game shut itself off, the computer screen going back to Alexandra's desktop. Hesitant, she looked at her brother, saw tears in his mysterious eyes, and noticed her eyes stung too, sniffling.

"I'm Kat," he said, quietly. "She is me." He put the mouse and microphone on the low table, picked up a Sweet Tart, only to put it back down.

***

Ben didn't know where to look. He fixed his eyes on the hardwood floor. Wiped away a tear that wanted to slip down his face. Unsure about what to do with his hands, he hugged himself. "She's me," he repeated. He wished numbness would take over, like it did when he was furiously studying for tests and ignoring the past. But it had finally caught up with him. He didn't know how to handle it. His gaze went to Alex, and he pleaded silently for something that would make him feel okay. But his thoughts wandered to that night.

Tricia

Tricia would never have left the house for so long by herself. Even if she *had* run away because she was angry at them for ignoring her. There was something terribly wrong. Alex had begged him to wait for the police and their parents to arrive before searching. She wanted more people at hand to help. But Ben had waited long enough. They had flashlights. He knew where they had to go. The police cars and an ambulance appeared, his parents soon after. They all got out of their cars.

Ben hopped into his old BMW without a word. Alex was already in it. She looked frightened but determined. Ben started the car and backed out of the driveway. Alex rolled down her window. "We're going to the woods behind the river!" she told anyone who was listening.

He imagined half of the policemen would stay at the house to investigate her room and the other half would come with them.

He had to keep his anger under control when he saw his father get back into his own car to follow the search party.

Bullshit he thought. *Don't start pretending to care.* Ben floored it and lost the police cars from view. He was at the river in top speed. They started the search on their own, the police close behind. Ben passed through the shallow part of the river as quickly as the water would allow. He glanced over his shoulder to see his twin sister follow. They were almost side-by-side. They went into the woods with their flashlights, started calling her name.

"Tricia!" Ben yelled.

"Trish!" called Alex.

"Patricia!" the closest policeman yelled.

"Patty!" their mom called out. Tricia hated that nickname.

They went deeper into the woods, shining their potent flashlights into trees, bushes, alcoves. They let moonlight do the rest.

"Split up," he told Alex. By now Tricia would've yelled back if she were able to. "We might find her faster." Alex nodded. Ben was about to go deeper in when he stopped to think. His little sister would never disobey his orders of going into the woods. She trusted him. Their initial premise was wrong. Maybe she hadn't run away out of anger after all. Maybe she was bored and had wanted to play.

"Where are you going?" Alex asked when she noticed him run in the opposite direction.

"The river!" he yelled back. He was back to the water quick, calling her name all the while. Ben shone his flashlight into her favorite trees. She used to collect flowers and beetles up there. He saw her stuffed rhino, partially hidden, in a taller tree. The police must've missed it since they didn't know where to look. "Alex!" Ben screamed. "Over here!"

Ben shone his light through the bushes under the tree. He

parted some bushes and saw her shoe. "Trish! Trish!" She must've lost her balance and fallen. He looked behind the bush and saw her laying there. There was a lot of blood coming from the back of her head, where it rested against a rock. It soaked through her dirty-blond hair and reached her pink backpack. Her arms were splayed, and her leg was at an odd angle. She must be in a lot of pain. He laid the flashlight on the ground, beside the rock.

"Ben," Tricia whispered.

"Shhhhhh… it's okay," he said to her. He sat down beside her face as easily as the underbrush would allow. Ben held one of his little sister's hands in both of his, stroking it. It was becoming colder. "We need a doctor!" he cried out. *Please let them be close,* he thought.

Alex was next to him in a split second. She approached Tricia slowly. Ben looked at his twin's face, anguish in the moonlight. But then Alex parted a smile and crouched down. "Heya, shrimp," she said.

"Hi," the girl replied weakly between labored breaths. "I knew it," she whispered out.

"Knew what, baby?" said Alex. A cry was audible in her voice. She came closer down, to look at Tricia. Alex held the shoed foot in her hand. The little girl had her eyes half-closed.

"Knew what, Trish?" said Ben, trying to keep her conscious.

"That you'd find me," she managed to say. Her voice was peaceful, like she knew this was the end.

"Yes," Ben said. "Yes, we found you."

"I was scared," said Tricia, and took a breath, "but you found me."

"I'm so sorry, Trish," Ben said, voice soft. "Tricia." She was silent. Her hand was ice cold. Ben checked for a pulse on her wrist. The little girl was gone.

He felt Alex's hand on his elbow. Ben heard people wadding through the river and the sound of hurried footsteps against dirt. His parents and police had arrived.

"Patricia!" cried her mother. "Benjamin, let me hold her. She needs me," she said.

"You're too late," Ben said. He looked up from his sister's little face. Rage enveloped him. "You're too late!" he yelled at his mother. "For everything! Don't pretend like you ever *fucking* cared. She's dead and you were too late to find her."

His mother's mouth was open in surprise. He was never one to yell, especially at his parents, but this was too much. Nothing mattered now but her lifeless hand in his own warm ones. He squeezed it tightly, hoping he would wake up from this nightmare.

"Do not speak to your mother like that," his father said, voice booming above the gurgle of the river. "She is our daughter. Now let us through."

"No," Ben said. They were ignoring his grief and he hated them for it. He closed his eyes to stop tears, but they kept coming. He felt Alex's hand on his shoulder. He looked up at her. "Alex," he uttered. His twin gently pried his hands away from Tricia's. She made him stand.

Their mother rushed to her youngest child. The police and paramedics gathered around the body.

"We did all we could, Ben," Alex said, soothing. She guided him away from the river to his waiting car. She drove him home in absolute silence.

***

His anger came roaring back. He tried to stop the tears from spilling out. Guilt shook him and he finally cried for her again. He was still looking at Alex, but his eyes were vacant, blurry. He saw her reach out to him and he welcomed her hug, though he couldn't muster to return it. "I should've been a better brother," he heard himself say. "I should've... should've focused on her that night, rather than my stupid PSAT. She deserved more. She deserved a better part... a better part of me," he managed.

"There, there," Alex was saying, "bring your tears to me. Don't face them alone." Tears were in her own voice and yet she was consoling him. He put his arms loosely around her, weeping.

"I should've been more," Ben said. "I should've talked to her. Maybe then she wouldn't have gone."

"You couldn't have stopped her even if you tried."

"Then I should've gone with her." He released his twin sister and she let go too. He got up and looked at her more closely. Her eyes had started to go red. He sniffled one last time. "I should've been there for when she lost her balance. I could've done something," he said, waving a hand in desperation.

"How could you have known?" his sister said, empathy in her voice. He wasn't sure what to do with empathetic Alex, but maybe that's what he needed right now. So, he accepted it. "How could either of us predict she was going to leave the house that night?" She was pleading for him to see some sense, but he had a hard time doing so. Ages of guilt, rage, and grief had taken hold of him, and they wouldn't let go that easily.

"Then Mom and Dad should've done a better job," he said as he started to pace the room.

Anger was bubbling up inside of him. He hugged himself to try to contain it. "We practically raised her. How can they call themselves parents?" He looked at Alex, expecting to see anger

213

in her face, too. But there was none.

"Their wrong was absence, not anything concrete," she said, dismissing Ben's thought with a hand. She smiled a small smile at him, and he knew she was trying hard to keep him from blowing up. He knew he was getting deadly close to doing so.

"Absent enough not to know where to look for her."

"But you did. You found her," she said, pleading in her voice. She extended a hand to him, probably to try to stop him pacing, but he wasn't done talking. She brought her hand back to herself.

"I never told you, did I?" He stopped pacing for a second to compose himself some. "I wake up thinking about her, still," Ben said, overwhelmed.

"I think about her all the time, too." Her eyes had started to glisten. But to his surprise, she let out a short laugh. "Why do you think I don't let you call me Alex anymore? She called me that, too." Alex sighed. "I even kept her stuffed rhino." She picked Scottie, the rhino, up from the table, where she had left it a few days ago. So maybe Alex did understand. He finally saw her grief. He decided it was okay to open up about his own some more.

He looked at the hardwood floor, not wanting to look into her eyes. "I kept her diary, as if reading it could change the past," he said, sniffling. "But nothing can, can it?" He glanced at her. She put a rogue strand of hair behind her ear.

"No, Ben," she said, "nothing can. We need to stop trying." Ben chuckled drily. He pointed at her. "You need to too, huh."

"Like you said, I let go of my dreams. I felt like I shouldn't try to be happy following my dreams after she was gone. I needed to learn to be there for people, because of what happened. Not teach people how to dance," she said, throwing up her hands. "If we had known what she wanted from us, rather than focus on ourselves, we might've been able to be there for her," she finished and hugged the stuffed rhino to her chest.

"I was reading her diary," he pointed at it, where it still kept the table balanced. "She wanted to talk to us about her bullying that day. And we ignored her."

"Do you think she left to be alone because she was upset we didn't give her attention? Either way, where is the line between our responsibility and hers?" Alex said. She put the rhino down beside her. "That question has plagued me ever since she left us. I haven't been able to find an answer." She looked down at her lap sadly.

"Psychologist hasn't helped?" he said and almost sat back down. Almost. Instead, he walked around the table, close to the TV.

"I stopped going to one when they threw the question back to me," she said, looking at him. He looked away, uneasy on his feet. "Not even the professionals know," he heard her continue. He looked up at her. "What I've come to accept is that she made her own choices," his twin said, one of her hands going straight down on her lap for emphasis. "She decided not to talk to us." She started enumerating on her fingers. "She decided to leave the house alone, whatever the reason. Decided to wear those shoes when I'd already told her not to."

"And we decided not to be there for her," Ben huffed at her. He walked his way around the left side of the table and stopped.

"She gave us nothing to be there *for*," Alex argued. She looked down at her lap, letting her thoughts flow. "Yes, I could've stopped talking to my childish boyfriend and talked to her about life. I made the decision not to and it was the wrong one, but that can't be the only reason she left that night. She left alone because she had longed to do so for a while. She found the opportunity

215

and she took it." She looked up at him again and her eyes were earnest.

"But I put both earphones in, Alex," he protested, "when I had promised her I wouldn't. I didn't realize I did until she was already gone." He looked down in shame.

"Did you make her go?" he hear Alex say.

"Well, no," he scratched his ear, thinking, "when you put it that way, I didn't."

"You were there for her, in her final moments." Alex had a wane smile on her face. "We both were. I have to keep telling myself that that's what matters, not our mistakes. We can't change those, but we can change how we react to them."

"She knew I'd find her. She even said so," Ben said, tears returning to his eyes. He fought against them and walked back, to be close to the TV yet again.

"That's being a good brother," Alex concluded, "and that reality trumps feeling like a bad one."

Ben glanced at the TV, then at his sister. "And I have to live with that."

"Not just live with it but thrive with it." She was pleading with him yet again.

"You should go back to dance," he said, rubbing his eyes to look at her clearly, across the table. "I think she would've been happy with it."

"I always thought…" Alex said, putting her thinking face on. Then she came back to reality. "I always thought I was being selfish for wanting to find happiness by teaching my passion to others. But you might have a point there." She smiled a little.

"I bet you're still super awkward around your clients at Love & Flowers," he said, and walked toward her to sit down on the sofa beside her.

She laughed. "Yes, yes I am. I'm surprised my boss hasn't fired me."

"Because it's you being you. You still get results, don't you? Your own way." He was seated now, calmer than he had been before he had opened up to her. The dam had been broken and it wasn't as bad as he thought it would be.

"Yes. My own way," she answered. "See here," she said, putting up a finger, moving in her seat so she was facing him, "I'll teach dance if you promise to look for a proper job, something in your area that *isn't* dishwashing."

"You saw that tab, huh." He raked his hand through his hair.

"Yes, and you should be ashamed," she said, and he saw a smile tugging at her lips. She couldn't even keep a straight face when accusing him.

But he wasn't the only one trying to circumvent the past, to live with it rather than thrive. "You can't tell me truthfully that you bought *Comatose* as anything other than a distraction from the elephant in the room."

"At first I thought I wanted to disrupt your peace," she said with a frown, putting her finger down. "Deep down I knew I was buying what I hoped would be a distraction. But it disrupted the peace after all."

Ben finally smiled. "Oddly enough, it did." He frowned. "Wonder how that happened." He thought for a second. Then he smiled again. "Either way, I'm glad it did."

"Are you?" she said, wringing her hands on her lap. "I thought you were going to blame me for getting back in touch with your emotions."

"It wasn't your fault. It was Kat's. I blame her," he pointed to the TV. Again, that nagging feeling came, the one that made him creeped out by Jack, as if he had somehow been listening to them whenever the game wasn't paused. He had a hard time pushing the thought aside.

Alex was smiling wide. "Fair enough," she said. Her eyes were hopeful when she said, "Questions. May I?"

He sighed. He had known this was coming. "Fire away," he said.

"Do you own... pajamas?"

Ben chuckled and shifted in his seat to look at her straight on. "I finally let you ask questions and that's your first one?" He couldn't help but grin at his twin.

"Just answer the question," she said, decidedly.

"Yes... but they need to be washed." He closed his eyes in preparation for her response.

"Ew!"

"Hey!" he said, snapping his eyes open, almost telling her that it was just how guys were.

She quickly walked away from her disgust. "Okay, okay, next question." She looked like a puppy with a juicy bone. He decided not to mention it. "Why... is your car filthy?"

"It isn't that bad! Just a couple of chips bags..." He put up two fingers. Two. Two wasn't that bad.

"And crumbs," she added for him.

"And crumbs." Ben had to smile.

"You'll get ants!" she protested.

"What do you want me to do, clean it out now?" he said, already getting up.

"No. I still have more questions." She put a hand on his arm to stop him. He sat back down and braced himself for the next one. "If I talked to Dad, would you let him use his connections to find you a job in chemical engineering?"

"You? Talking to Dad?" he asked in disbelief.

"I'd do it for my favorite brother." She smiled.

He chuckled. "Let me search for myself some more."

Alex wrinkled her nose at that. "Have you been searching for anything other than dishwashing jobs? Tell me truly," she said, accusation creeping up in her voice.

"I already told you I applied for an engineering one," he said, refusing to look her in the eye. He didn't have enough experience to get the job.

She huffed. "Okay, I want to argue about that one, but I won't."

"Thank you," he replied, genuine. The coast was clear, so he looked at her again.

She wasn't done. "How far have you gotten in your new Kurt Vonnegut book?" she asked. "Get past chapter one?"

Ben reached over to pick the book up from the floor. "I actually planned on reading some right now. If your majesty is done prodding."

"I am not," she said, putting up an index finger.

"Yes...?" He raked a hand through his hair.

"Next question." Ben wondered what this one could possibly be. He waited. "Why did you feel guilty? I know, I know, you should've done more for her, you should've stopped her. But... but that doesn't mean you're guilty."

"I didn't protect her." He was getting exasperated.

"Dad and Mom were meant to protect her. Not you. You were only sixteen. She wasn't your kid."

"Wasn't she, though? Didn't we raise her?" he asked, and tears were starting to come to his eyes again. He wasn't sure if he was okay with this.

"Ben. It wasn't our job." She touched his arm with hesitant fingers, as if she didn't know if she was allowed to console him.

"She was our little sister," he said, getting more upset than anything.

"Sister. Not daughter."

Ben huffed. "Didn't you feel guilt, too?" He was very curious about this and eyed her closely.

"About talking to Brenden and making her leave my room?"

"Yeah, that."

"I did. I certainly did," she said, a frown on her face due to remembering. "For a while I couldn't live with myself."

"What helped? You said the psychologist didn't." In the five years he had dealt with the loss of Tricia, he had refused to see a therapist, no matter how many people urged him to do so.

"The psychologist did help, to a certain point," Alex said to his surprise. "I wonder if I would've gotten to the conclusion that it wasn't my fault faster if I had gone to another one." At this, she looked down at her hands. But just as quickly, she looked back up at him. "Instead, I told myself every morning, 'She's gone. It wasn't your fault.'"

"Just that?" It couldn't be just that.

"That, and talking to my wise friend Frannie. She was the only other person I had told about what happened. I should get back in touch with her..." Alex made a face. "I kind of stopped."

"What did she tell you?" Ben asked urgently. Alex smiled.

"What I'm telling you."

"Oh," he said. "Thought you were all life-smart," Ben said playfully.

"Hey! I *am* smart. I listened." She pointed that accusing finger at him. "You should, too."

"I am!"

Alex closed her eyes and sighed. "You need time to heal," she said. "I need patience."

Her amber eyes were fixed on his again. He was getting familiar with her stare again, not feeling accused by it like he had felt ever since he had come to stay with her. Did this mean he was healing?

He was about to ask her that but instead clung onto her confession. "Yes," he agreed. "You always were the impatient one." He smiled so she wouldn't think he was getting at her for it. "I remember you almost broke your ankle trying to do a pirouette the day you got your dance shoes."

To his surprise, she laughed. "I had forgotten about that," she said.

He smiled. "I will never let you forget."

"You really shouldn't." She faced forward again. "Okay, I'm done. You may read."

"Thank you kindly." He faced forward as well. She gave him a soft punch on the arm. Then, she picked up her laptop and started browsing the internet.

It finally felt right to be in the same room with her, just like the days before Tricia's accident. He felt a twinge of missing and looked at her diary under the table leg. Then he shook his head and got comfortable on the sofa to read.

***

The voices have left me. I am in darkness, alone. I curl up in a fetal position on the cold floor. Is this what I'm here for? To help others heal with my pain? My suffering has not been in vain, then. Maybe someday someone else will pick up my game. Maybe I will help those people as well. Did I help Benjamin and Alex? I'm not sure. They seemed to listen intently to all I had to say. And I helped them by bringing up certain memories and putting them

221

in order when they asked for it. They weren't with me all the way through, however. They took Solstice away from me a few times; some of them completely, others temporarily. I'm still new to this, to this type of help. The last time I was in Solstice was ten years ago – each year punctuated by a dim light that disappeared as quickly as it appeared – and the last people I helped sounded too young and inexperienced in life to be helped and to help. I remember a name; Luke... Luke was his name.

But I wasn't able to teach them anything. I have a feeling they will pick me up again and I will again be of use again. All I can do is wait. Farewell for now, readers.